EROS

ADULT FICTION

Into the Black

David Aaron Clark

Series editor: Maxim Jakubowski

INTO THE BLACK

ISBN 1 85286 679 9

Series editor: Maxim Jakubowski

Published by Eros Plus
An imprint of Titan Books
42-44 Dolben Street
London SE1 0UP

First UK edition November 1996
1 3 5 7 9 10 8 6 4 2

British Library Cataloguing-in-Publication Data. A catalogue record for this book is available from the
British Library.

Printed and bound in Great Britain by Cox and Wyman Ltd, Reading, Berkshire.

Dedicated to Howard Thompson and Jobbe Eagle, two very dear and faithful friends who did more than their part to keep me sane long enough to finish this fucker.

And at evening let them return: and let them make a noise like a dog, and go round about the city.
Let them wander up and down for meat, and grudge if they be not satisfied....
Consume them in wrath, consume them, that they may not be:
And let them know that God ruleth in Jacob until the ends of the earth.
Psalm 59

For if the word spoken by angels was steadfast and every trans-gression and disobediance recieved a just recompense of reward; how shall we escape, if we neglect so great a salvation?
The epistle of Paul to Philemo

Jesus, help me find my proper place.
The Velvet Underground

I

*t*he repetition was numbing, except to her arm, which was becoming sore.

Sweat stung her eyes, made her fear for her eyeliner, thanks to the faulty air-conditioning. The big, outdated machine blurted industrial wheeze from the corner where it lurked, alternating jets of warm air that felt sick with virus and shudder-inducing blasts of muddy ice cold.

Mistress Medusa stared fixedly at the wispy black hair coiled on the nape of the man she was beating, seeking some abstract *satori* that would carry her through another session. *Ah, money, the root of it all.* Or the love of money, was the exact quote.

I would do anything for love, but I won't do that, a blandly tortured AOR singer softly bleated from the boom box on top of the air conditioner, the lyric jumping out at her in sharp relief. Medusa, known off-duty to friends, lovers and the telephone company as Mary Ellen Masters, rolled her eyes and thought about the lonely routine of returning to an empty apartment.

It didn't have to be empty. Billy, the slave due to pick her up at the end of the shift, was handsome in an unlined boy-next-door sort of way. Unfortunately he owned the cognitive abilities — and aptitude for pouting — of an eleven-year-old. But then who else could she count on to come pick her up at one a.m. on Christmas Eve?

Even though Medusa was only five years older than Billy — not yet quite thirty herself — she too often felt like a horny, corrupt old witch, confronting his childish, muscular simplicity. He reminded her of Lenny from *Of Mice and Men*.

Especially when she'd tie him down to her bedroom floor and tease him with her naked ass, swaying it inches from his gaping mouth, the meat of it pulled apart by her sunken-in red nails to reveal the brown wink of her asshole. Or when she'd step on his hard cock with her stiletto heel, grinding into the main vein in sharp half-circles until tears came to his eyes.

She wondered if she took advantage of him. But hey, if it wasn't her, it would end up being some other mistress who might really fuck him over.

She noticed that her client was shivering, and not from the rain of blows she was delivering. She dreaded the inevitable complaint about the climate inside the dungeon. What was she supposed to do? The Manager was in the back, snorting cocaine with a bunch of rock 'n' roll transvestites and other drug-hungry hangers-on, the whole brood kept watch over by Stubby, the burly black bodyguard in muscle t-shirt and cowboy hat who popped up to lend immoral support whenever The Manager was feeling particularly paranoid. The Manager was the one who was supposed to keep the place in decent repair.

"Can't we do something about the air-conditioning?" the client whined. She winced at the chalky slide of her teeth gritting. She absolutely hated it when clients whined. As if she didn't have enough fucking problems in the world.

She kept her composure, though.

"Now, you know I told you I'd do what I could last time, but how much trouble do you want to put your mistress through? Isn't it a slave's place to suffer?"

"Only the way he wants to, when he's paying."

You fucking asshole. She strode up behind him, grabbed a handful of hair and pulled his head back so he could see the white-hot chill in her narrowed eyes, the exaggerated flare of nostrils made so artificially elegant by a plastic surgeon's hand.

"I'll see what I can do."

She slammed the dungeon door behind her and leaned on it for a moment and exhaled deeply, shoulders slumped. Sasha, the other mistress on duty, looked up from her copy of a French fashion magazine. She had violet eyes, narrow and heavily lashed, framed by thick eyeliner that ended on either side of her face in vaguely Egyptian squiggles.

"Tough one? Old Eddie acting up?"

"It's the fucking air conditioning. What's it doing on in December, anyway?"

Sasha winced, squinching up her nose. She laid the magazine down on her naked stomach, a flat pale expanse that ran from the bottom of her chain-mail bra all the way to the waist of her black leather skirt.

"Got to every few hours. No circulation in this fucking hole. That room's stuffy all year round. I hate it."

"It doesn't bother me."

"The haunted room."

"Yeah, right, I heard about that. Pair of feet?"

"Jennie, the manager's old girlfriend, claimed she saw them at 3.30 in the morning when she staying over alone one night."

"Whatever. I've got to deal with this."

The Manager was sprawled on a black leather divan, his air force flight suit complemented by a sad, haunted look around the hollows of his sunken-in eyes, and the two-day stubble gristled against his taut cheekbones.

Medusa noted the open magazine on the coffee table, spine up. In the shadow between page and highly polished Formica glinted the signature glass straw he used in the ongoing demolition work he was perpetrating against his nasal cavity.

"My client's complaining about the air-conditioning again."

The Manager shifted uncomfortably on his ass, favouring the leg that bulged through the jumpsuit at the thigh, where there was a day-old dressing wrapped over a recent bullet wound. She hated it when he was in shorts and she had to stand there and wait for him to process a credit card number, with nothing to stare at except the quarter-sized yellow stain in the cotton bandage marking the slowly healing wound.

"Tell him it's a slave's place to suffer."

"I did. He didn't buy it."

The hangers-on that filled the room looked about uncomfortably, not wanting to be drawn into the controversy, or to be reminded what it was like to work for The Manager rather than just loiter about and help him do his drugs. Stubby gingerly picked up The Manager's ferret and drew him close to his face, making a project of attempting to stare the beady-eyed creature down. She couldn't decide which beast looked less clever.

"Well, Jesus, *Mistress*," The Manager punched the word with sarcastic emphasis, "I don't *know*. Handle it. It's your session. I called the repairman twice, but he never showed. And here I am trying to have an important business conference with my associates about some new creative projects that might bring us all, including you, more money, and you're bothering me because you can't deal with some pathetic slave of a client bitching at you?"

Stomping by Sasha on the way back in, Medusa met the other girl's inquiring eyes with a vicious shrug and the usual prayer: "I hope to God that fuckhead ODs!"

When she got back to the dungeon the client was seated on the rough wooden bench, lacing up his shoes. His pants were already back on. His white shirt lay unbuttoned and sagging open, displaying the smooth paunch of his belly. She chuckled to herself — slouched down to reach his shoestrings like that, he almost looked pregnant.

"Look, I'm really sorry, I did what I could," she apologised, feeling exceedingly stupid standing there in the middle of the room in her leather corset and thigh-highs, all dressed up with no place to land her blows.

"It's okay. Keep the money. I'll just have to ask when I call next time to see if the air-conditioning's working right. Or else just go somewhere else."

Do that, bastard. In a way, she was almost relieved to end the session early, even if it meant possibly losing a regular. This regular was predictably arrogant and unpleasant, always demanding and complaining, hardly the soul of a submissive. Always wanting to see her tits, and trying to get her to let him lick them, too.

He buttoned his shirt and stood up to stuff it into his pants. Looking at his weak chin, his petulant eyes, she smiled. He'd be back, anyway. She had his number. She had all the clients' numbers. They shared the same exchange.

Sasha's shift ended at midnight; when Medusa left an hour later, the dungeon would actually close down for twenty four hours, as The Manger drank and snorted his way into an even thicker stupor than usual.

Sasha waved goodbye, making a quiet escape in order to thwart his keen hearing; he would have insisted she come to the back for a holiday line of blow, and she was trying to stay mostly clean. Medusa was sucking at the bottom of a waxy cup of iced coffee, her third of the evening. She'd hoped the caffeine would keep her awake, but somehow she was still nodding off, only now her teeth ground against themselves even as her chin headed for the promisingly pillow-white expanse of her chest.

As she slipped between states, her gaze focused and unfocused on the set of African ceremonial masks on the wall, another of The Manager's psycho art touches. Their multi-coloured stares were fierce, empty eyeholes full of nothing but shadow and maybe that doorway to the plane of unreason where restless spirits and malevolent angels flew in circles, seeking a pathway into reality, where they could commit the sort of chaos and atrocity that was their food.

Something on the wall moved. Starting, she threw her head back and woke up. Just a dream, a shadow, a misfiring synapse.

What a place to spend Christmas Eve.

But with rent nearly due and her credit card balance still suffering from that last extravagant trip to Wicked Pleasures — the iridescent violet latex sheath dress and matching boots and riding crop had come to over $700 — here she sat, g-string digging into the crack of her ass. And an old, smelly g-string to boot — Alex, the Rolex-wearing shit freak with the receding hairline, had called to schedule for today, and he always tipped her $100 for the juiciest, most stained underthings she could supply. Of course he hadn't shown up. Doubtless doing some last minute gift-shopping for his wife.

The phone was ringing sporadically, the usual crew of phone freaks reduced in strength somewhat by actual alternative activities, be it busing home to the folks out on the Island or drowning their loneliness in front of a beer tap. Bill the Floor called to inform her he was spending Christmas Eve rolled up in a castoff rug by the main entrance to Macy's, where all the shoppers would be forced to tread on him on their way in and out. He asked her if she would bail him out if he were arrested. She laughed and hung up on him.

Slave Milton called, too, wanting to reminisce about the time she'd had him dress in his best garters and stockings and suck her boyfriend's cock while she sodomised him. Nostalgia for that particular escapade did not run high for her; that boyfriend had been a near-perfect asshole. She'd found him in the filthy bathroom of an East Village bar with some mascara-poisoned goth bitch attached to his dick by her gaping mouth. When she'd flung open the door, he'd gazed at her stupidly, as if to say, "*I* don't know how she got there!"

When the phone rang at quarter to twelve, she thought it would be Milton or Bill again. Instead it was a unknown male voice, anonymous under a sheen of street noise and static. Calling from a phone booth.

"Hello, I was hoping to make a last-minute appointment."

"Have you been here before?"

There was a hesitation that made her sigh: another creep.

"No, not actually, but I'm familiar with the place, and with you, Mistress Medusa. I saw your ad in *Domina Directory*, and everybody says you're the best mistress in New York City."

Oh please. The shameless lines they fed you. Still, *Domina Directory* was a speciality magazine, the sort you had to go to a particular kind of store to find, and it was not cheap.

"Well, it *is* late, you know, we were about to close."

"Oh please, Mistress. I promise to make it worth your while. I'll bring you a gift."

She ticked off the possibilities: bad cocaine, half-dead flowers from the Korean bodega down the block, some ugly piece of St. Mark's junk jewellery. Still, the rent, the rent. No sessions so far tonight. Cat food, even. Okay. The Manager wouldn't even realise how late it was until she brought him back his cut after it was all over but the screaming.

"All right. You have five minutes to be at the door. Any later and I'm not answering. Do you know where you're going? Where are you?"

"I know where to come."

She went back and informed the Manager there was a last client on his way in. Just to be contrary, he complained about having to operate on Christmas day, though she knew he was more greedy for the money than she was. She gave him a calculatedly helpless what-can-you-do look and went to reapply her makeup in the cramped bathroom. Since it hadn't been cleaned by a house slave since the night before, she was economical about brushing any exposed skin against its surfaces.

When the buzzer went off she bumped her knee against one of the skinny silver legs holding up the orange-stained sink, and cursed, even though the leather of her boot muffled any real sting.

He was actually pretty handsome.

She thought for sure that only a troll would come creeping in at such a ridiculous moment, in the fleeting moments before the day of Christ's birth, good will toward men, peace on earth, all that rot. But what the fuck, that was a nice head of hair he had, long and smooth, brown and blonde like in a shampoo commercial, sort of a well-groomed rock star look, just on the verge of tumbling too far over into pretty boy but not quite.

The goatee was trendy and appropriate, too, emphasising the angularity of his cheeks, the long thinness of his nose. His blue eyes wove spells of gentle fascination in the air, as he gazed forthrightly into her own brown eyes. She felt like she was looking into a three-dimensional greeting card, a Midwestern Protestant version of Jesus. *Jesus, have you come to save me?* she thought, transforming her amusement into a smile of greeting.

"Hello," he said warmly, without embarrassment.

"This way to the dungeon," Medusa said, and smiled as she stood aside to let him pass, straightening her back so her breasts stood higher on her ribcage.

Once in the room she instructed him to strip while he told her his scene. This was the part she sometimes dreaded, when the gross, angry things that went beyond the mere animal and into the black hopelessness of addictive depravity reared their reptilian heads and hissed thick cremes of poisoned hormone and past trauma at her. It was a new episode — several times a day if her bank account was lucky — of "Welcome to My Fetish": *Hi there*, could you tell I was a piss freak, a toe sucker, a navel-licker, an asshole sniffer, a shit eater, an aspiring transvestite, a mommy's boy who wants daddy to sodomise him, a nigger slave in need of a good and bloody beating from the mistress of the house, a guilt-eaten Jew begging to be fucked in the mouth and ass with the stiletto heel of a black-raincoated SS officer?

"I think a scourging is in order, Mistress," Jesus said, a sad smile drawing his upper lip underneath the soft-looking hair decorating it. Without being asked, he handed her two still-crisp hundred dollar bills, which she tucked into the top of her boot. She wondered if he was a good fuck.

"I think you'd better face the wall, then, slave," she replied without even having to consider, stepping as she spoke towards the equipment rack. Many of the pieces were secured by bicycle chains. You were supposed to check out the keys at the beginning of your session, to cut down on theft, which the Manager claimed ran into the tens of thousands per year.

Wrinkling her nose at being reminded of The Manager, she used the bobby-pin she kept stuck in her bra to spring the tumblers on the small gold lock installed on her favourite rubber whip's handle.

It was late; that was why she would start with the rubber. Billy would be here soon, and though she usually took pleasure in keeping him waiting as long as possible, tonight she just wanted to get out of this constricting place and…where? Home? To have to watch Billy jerk off on his knees at her feet before she pushed him whining out the door so she could watch TV alone until she fell asleep on the couch? To a bar, to drink with losers, where everyone could see she had no steady boyfriend, no family or friends she cared for enough to be with?

The rubber lash arced and snapped down so perfectly it barely made a whisper before stopping short with a loud, sharp snap against the client's shoulderblades.

He quivered once, then stood his ground. This was sick, on Christmas Eve. But she was going to enjoy it.

After five minutes of working him over, she had driven his knees nearly but not quite to the Burmese carpet. The battle between their force of wills made her aware of her pussy in a very itchy, insistent way. She felt the seam of her red plastic g-string slide against her crotch, catching against the outer folds of her vulva, freshly shaven that morning.

"So you're a tough little slave, huh. I'll bet you're always begging to be beaten, crawling around on your hands and knees looking for a beautiful woman to whale the shit out of you."

"I am here because I should be."

"You're so right, you — " she stopped, distracted by a warm breeze brushing her back, abrupt but welcome in the dungeon's refrigerated chill. Thinking The Manager or one of his stupid, coked-up flunkies had barged in, she spun around, angry invective already boiling on her tongue.

The blue door was still secure, but wriggling there in front of it was a baby in a pink diaper. A delicate web of black follicles glossed the egg-shaped head. When the spit-glittered slash of a mouth began to curl open, Medusa found herself torn between deep instincts to rush forward in maternal concern as well as coil back in primal terror.

An oversized tongue slowly unrolled from within the foundling's mouth, a black scaly phallus split at the end into a pair of greasy pink antennae, like one found on a slug.

In the shadows beneath the child's cheeks, she detected a row of wormy white legs sprouting a few centimetres out of the flesh, imbuing the face with a subtle animation, a soft blur.

She averted her gaze, head snapping away as if she'd been slapped. A weightless terror rippled up swiftly from her feet, disappearing into a tight cubbyhole somewhere inside her head. She looked back and was confronted by a bare spot on the floor, bland and sure of its own innocence.

The client was still facing the wall, the muscles embracing his slim skeleton insinuatingly evident under his thin, nearly golden skin. She buried her shock in an avalanche of resentment for his beauty, and shoved his face forward until it rebounded from the wall against her gloved palm. She brushed his hair aside with her nose so she could crunch her teeth nearly together through the brittle lobe of his ear.

"You know you're keeping the mistress from important matters with your petty need to be punished," she whispered to him. That was it. Concentrate on the script, play the scene, live the part and don't worry if you're suddenly prone to acid flashbacks. It's not like it's *Jacob's Ladder* time or something. Next stanza.

"But that's what you want to do, isn't it? Make me angry, so I'll hurt you even more. You're all so predictable, I'm afraid. You're just like the rest. Pigs."

She dragged him over to the large wooden cross set against the south wall, varnished oak that gleamed with ten thousand moments of hired pain, a thousand different men's fetish-wrapped passion plays. In moments of boredom when there were no clients, and no other mistresses around, she would bend down and lightly kiss it, imagining she could taste the dark vibrations.

Quickly binding his wrists and ankles with the leather restraints chained to the cross, Medusa then squatted down before his cock and wrapped it neatly with a leather cord procured from her belt. When she was done, a series of black coils squeezed it so tightly that the head was of twice greater diameter than the shaft. On the other end, the testicles were separated by a harsh set of loops that promoted a whisper of blue across a surface tension so overripe it was painful just to witness.

Then she stood back and laid into him with the red cat-of-nine-tails. Intent that he get his money's worth of suffering.

The slap of each blow was so sharp that its report was an affront unto itself, a brittle bark that set your teeth on edge. Each tongue of leather drummed against the flesh, and red welts eagerly dashed up to greet them. Ready to be transformed, ready to fuck with, ready to fuck, down to the atom.

Gentle moans spilled out of him, sexual in their careless intimacy, rising and falling in response to each lash. Infected by his passion, Medusa luxuriated in the bristling static travelling the circuit between them.

When she struck him harder, the cries grew in intensity but not volume. Pleasant. His features were drawn taut, an elegant mask begging to be shattered. Harder.

The first dash of blood was unexpected, a brief smear across his ribs that was dispersed with the next blow. Then two more appeared, and soon it looked like red paint across his torso. She had rarely beaten somebody this badly, and certainly never without discussion beforehand. What drove her now?

As soon as she questioned it the compulsion dissipated, and she found herself rubbing her sore shoulder. The urge to apologise gripped her, until she saw that the client was smiling at her in a loving but mocking manner, presuming empathy with a stranger. What ego these bastards had!

"Slave. Nothing to say for yourself? Shall I whip you some more?"

"Do what you will." A politely delivered challenge.

She stalked forward and forced open his mouth. Turning her face as if to kiss him, she instead filled his mouth with an eruption of foamy spittle.

She stepped back to strike him again, but paused to watch her saliva pour back out over his lip, riding a wave of some amber liquid wallowing up from his throat, a greasy-looking resin that slopped down over his chest. It sizzled where it met bare flesh, and flared like sugar over a gas flame where there was blood and open wounds.

Blinded by the sudden, furious constellation, Medusa saw another vision.

A goat, coat matted with burrs, spiked with dirty spit curls. Its horns were ancient, so cracked they seemed as if they must be petrified, dry as dust except for a gelid smear at their centre. Between its heaving flanks, a forked cock dangled.

"Shame the devil," the client whispered encouragingly. She snapped out of the vision to see him hanging there by his wrists, limp and weary, his chest a red mess. She slapped him so hard her fingers stung, even inside her glove, and she felt her nails pushed back where his skin had caught against them and yielded up some of its own.

"Piss on the devil. And piss on you, you weird little fucking worm," she hissed, playing now not at all, excited in a way she'd never been during a session.

"It's time to take Mistress Medusa's fucking communion. My Christmas gift to you," she told him, twisting a nipple so greasy with blood it nearly slipped from between her fingers.

Unbuckling him from the cross, she didn't even bother to

massage his wrists to restore circulation. Instead she pushed him flat down on the carpet, and shinnied her leather g-string down across the swell of her hips and thighs, catching it briefly on the tops of her boots before slipping completely free of it. Conveniently, the crotch of her fishnet tights was already torn out; these were her work clothes.

She stood over him, her legs apart, eyes squeezed shut. She concentrated on the warmth above her hips, as her kidneys spasmed and released a hot, filling spray that came jetting out from between the lips of her vulva, cooling a few degrees in the open air before spattering in golden explosions all over her client's angular face, clear beads collecting in his beard and moustache. *They gave him vinegar to drink, mixed with gall.* The words came into her head — were they from the Bible?

When she looked down she screamed without sound, no air in her lungs to expel. There was a black funnel between her legs, wet and spinning, pulsing inside like the mouth of a snake. The glittering twist of her urine was quickly lost in its whirring hunger. When the funnel bumped its hot edge against her thighs, she fell faint for a moment, everything lost in a grey, hazy buzz.

When her vision cleared and thought returned she saw that what was bumping her thighs were the client's ears, and that his all-too human face was placidly braced against her cunt, only the faintest gurgling betraying the efficient drain of piss down his throat. In a gesture just short of inadvertent, her gloved hand brushed across her belly, PVC fingertips grazing the most upward jut of her clitoris. The pre-orgasmic wave that resulted was strangely welcome. She clamped her thighs tightly, smothering the client, the tension of the contracted muscles trailing a warm finger up her spine.

Then the world dropped away again and she was in a dark circus, surrounded by a listless jabbering crowd peppered with leering clowns. She was small and holding a big man's hand, rounded dry tips rasping against her soft little-girl palm, wishing he would pay attention, wishing he would stop talking to the lady with him, her and her big white boom-booms all spilling out of that purple dress.

The worst part was always afterwards, when he'd hold her tight on the subway ride home and whisper to her, his breath sour and unpleasant with the hint of some unimaginable bad thing, that this was just between them, right, their little secret, don't tell Mom, how about a soda pop, sweetie?

One of the clowns shuffled close and started making a fuss over her, patting her head and waving a pink balloon in front of her face. Dry fingers slipped from her hand and she lurched off-balance, a warm resistance covering her limbs as she fell into the clown's arms but they weren't arms, they were huge snakes of some sort, long white organs with pulsing veins that rose and fell across their wattled surface as if their entire widths were each a huge lung, or one vein throbbing with a mountain's stream of blood.

Hot to the touch against her face, the snakes contracted a moment before growing even larger, even as she felt more of them curling around her legs, spreading them apart; her waist, bracing it firmly; her arms, binding them.

Mary Ellen looked down at the floor, the leather harness limp around her high heels, waiting to be pulled up so it could hoist the large, realistic dildo resting loosely within its ring tight against her crotch. White angels danced mockingly over the shiny black surface of her boots.

Not only another hallucination, but now she was losing real time as well, during which her body could evidently act upon its own. Shit, this had to stop! Was it time to take a cab to Bellevue and check herself in?

Finish the session, just finish the fucking session. Make the asshole come and let him wipe his dick and put his clothes on and get the fuck out. No, don't even let him wipe his dick. Out. And then a sedative. There were a couple of Darvons knocking around in the bottom of her purse.

The harness fit snugly up the crack of her ass, and when the last buckle was secure she threw her shoulders back, adjusting to the extra weight with a flourish, happy to adopt an exaggerated male swagger from where she could feel safe and in control. Open up your asshole, asshole.

"Time to really get down to business, worm. Time to turn you into my little bitch, you're such a pretty little thing, you'll like that, won't you, I bet it won't be the first time for a slut like you."

The client looked at her with his peculiar eyes, and sighed.

"No, I suppose it won't," he agreed. His mouth turned down a bit, making him look something like a pouty rock star, soft hair coyly masking one cheek.

She bent him over the bondage table, his bloody chest pressed against the burnished ebony surface. Leaning against him, rubbing the shaft of the cock between his haunches, she removed her elbow-length gloves. Then she drew her nails sharply down from his shoulders to those haunches, leaving trails so deep that irregular beads of blood dotted the path. The client moaned in pain, his agony more musical than ever.

She pushed open his cheeks and fit the grease-smeared cock in the revealed depression there. She considered the mercy of gently working it in. Decided otherwise.

His head reared back howling when she penetrated him as abruptly and deeply as she could. The butt of the dildo pressed against her pubic mound, eliciting a jolt of pleasure. She drew her hips back so that the dildo eased nearly free, so that the flare of the corona popped out, and would have to be jammed back in.

Then she started to really fuck him.

She liked to count strokes. It was an idiosyncrasy of hers, a macho little thing. She lost count somewhere around a hundred.

Now she could feel the resistance ebbing and flowing as his sphincter spasmed open and shut, an involuntary reaction in no way dictated by his own pleasure. His cheek was pressed against the ebony table, his one visible eye gleaming from within twisted folds of skin, a geography of pain and humiliation distilled into the base language of the flesh.

She reached her arms out to rake his back, nails just freshly manicured that day digging their honed tips into the flesh again, digging and rending until more blood began to well up around them, a near match to the dark shade of enamel. His back and chest were now uniformly ravaged.

Mistress Medusa shuddered under the pressure of the gold ring she wore in her clitoral hood as it was pushed back by the dildo at the apex of its thrust.

As her orgasm approached — *an orgasm with a client?* she dimly thought, in some far compartment of her mind — the body beneath her began to transmute, turning thicker, saggier, the long brown meadow locks going brittle and pale, the top of the head emerging as the hair receded, an eclipse reversed.

The slim, hungry hips she had clutched disappeared in folds of loose skin, the golden cast changing to liver-spotted brown and white-pink, like exposed meat. The writhing muscles in the back disappeared in waves of rolling fat. Her slashes, however, remained, now looking so much crueller, so much more merciless, against the texture of this ugly, vulnerable skin.

Though she couldn't see the face, head hunched down between collapsed shoulders, her belly jumped with fear and the first faint whisper of hysteria. She recognised this man, by his body, his posture, by his scent. At the exact same moment she knew by the proof of her senses that it was him, her mind rebelled and told her why it could not be:

He had been dead for three years.

In fury, in desperation, trying to drive out this incarnation of the demon she was trapped in the room with, she fucked him harder, driving the rubber prong as deeply between his flabby haunches as her hips could shove it. So hard her thighs ached, standing as she was in these heels, and her head swam, and her belly ached as the moment of climax drew even nearer.

Just as the first rolls of white pleasure crashed over the vines of her nervous system, he, to her horror, spoke. Spoke in that voice that had read her "*The Cat in the Hat*," had scolded her for bad report cards, had whispered soothing sweetnesses to her in the middle of the night so she wouldn't scream and wake anybody up.

"Sweetie? I know it hurts. I'm sorry, it's my fault. You weren't a bad little girl. I loved you but I did something wrong."

Her orgasm broke in full force, a universe of ash congealing into grey jelly that burned and cleansed with the force of fifteen years of bad dreams and abusive boyfriends and bulimia and cocaine-fuelled orgies where somebody always came out bloody and a nervous laugh that could never be called happy and a granite death wish that weighed down the very pit of her heart, that only rushed forward in moments of extreme drunkenness or depression, but someday would surely have its way.

She squeezed her eyes until they ached, trying to stave off the river of tears that forked down either side her nose, meeting and pooling on the quivering ridge of her full upper lip. The sobs wracked her entire torso, wrenching and rippling against the equally strong twitches of her now singing clitoris.

She howled his name in two long syllables that seemed to turn her lungs inside out, a wail of anger and despair refining itself into a contralto of forgiveness and regret. She felt an incredibly perfect love, born in the warmth far underneath the flesh, in the faint electric charge bearing the particular flicker of one soul, that her life's entire experience seemed compressed into one beautiful, terrible, ultimately predestined moment of empty peace. She thought she had died.

Her eyes were still shut when she felt the pressure of his ass against her thighs vanish. The nimbus of blue flame that caressed her limbs and thickened into a crown around her head began to slowly wane.

Her spirit rattled in her bones, and the ride came to a stop. Opening her eyes, she surveyed the empty room before her. The air conditioner wheezed in the most stupid of ways.

Under its mechanical rhythm a whisper rose from the nothingness to teeter just on the edge of audibility, a voice without gender or inflection: "*This gift among others I give to thee, that thy sleep might be easier.*"

She knew she should be screaming, or praying, or banging her head against the wall until all memories of this vision retreated into an understandable reality. Instead she squatted there, rocked back on her compressed haunches, the oily black dildo dangling in its impotent greasy innocence like a child's sticky toy.

She began to hum to herself, to smile, when the warm wetness called her attention to the palms of her hands, from which blood had begun to weep. Somebody was banging on the door; dimly she heard Stubby's voice, and silly Billy's, too, frightened for her, confused.

She brought her palms close to her face, and inhaled deeply, hoping for a smooth copper high that would head off hysteria.

II

_____

*t*alk about your ravages of lust. His lips were as bruised as rotten fruit, his eyes two desert sinkholes with scorpions squirming in the pits, trying to avoid the light. You could have sliced open a finger on one of his cheekbones.

Appropriate enough for a would-be angel of death, Frank Breedlove decid planted on a park bench and watching the black teenager's approach from behind his mirrored sunglasses.

The kid walked with that shit-in-my-pants sidle that tough boys with soft, fearful centres like to affect, their pre-emptive strike against all the imagined unfriendly forces arrayed around them. One strap of his faded overalls drooled down over a sun-burnt shoulder, and he wore a Raiders cap backwards. Dennis the (public) Menace. Pockets full of brass and shit-brown buds of sense, or perhaps even petite, red-capped vials full of cola-coloured crystals.

Frank, a short man who looked indistinctly middle-aged,

slight jowls flecked with grey, sucked in the radical curve of his paunchy belly as best he could and stepped into the young panther's path.

"Hi, my name's Frank. Wanna kill me?"

"Gedoudamahway, man," the boy said, trying to avoid having to meet Frank's eyes. He took him for a lunatic to be brushed away, lest some hint of madness smear off and sink into his own flesh. Who else would challenge him like this on his own turf? Let this bugfuck bum live to drink his next pint of Night Train.

Frank placed a soft hand against the boy's chest, feeling the warm beat of his heart even through the thick denim of the overalls.

"What's wrong, you look tough enough to take me. Or are you really just a little shit-assed pussy-boy that Momma forgot to wipe?" Frank hissed at him, his wheezing voice cracking a little at the end of his breaths.

The words kindled an angry fire in the youth's eyes, and almost before Frank could see it, a blade flashed out and sunk in between his fourth and fifth ribs. He sighed, just to feel it grind against the bone. Good old friction. The kid stood staring at him expectantly, impatient for Frank's face to contort in pain, for him to crumple and fall to the grass.

Instead the portly little man reached out and grabbed the handsome face before him and offered it a hungry kiss, luxuriating in the full, warm lips that drew back in terror so that the two men's teeth clicked together. The small sound echoed in both their sets of bones. Frank tensed his stomach and forced the shiv back out. It clattered against the sidewalk.

"What are you, some kind of crazy cracked-up motherfucker?" the boy gasped, scrabbling against Frank's bony, pale hands, which were buried in the cloth of his overalls, keeping him a breath away. Frank smiled deferentially, and offered his best explanation.

"Don't pay me any mind. I'm just crazy from the heat, son. Don't worry, it won't hurt for long, and then you'll be food."

Frank let go and turned away without even granting the kid another look, not bothering to watch him stumble away, rubbing his lips so hard it seemed they would bleed. The little brat's world rocked.

By the time the kid makes it to the entrance of the park, Frank thought, he'll already be dissolving, his bones softening and running, his fluids evaporating up toward a pregnant rain cloud ready to recycle them onto the heads of the unwary and the unknowing.

Frank could still taste the gummy flavour of the boy's soul on his tongue. A quicker, even more unhealthy high than the MSGs in a carton of Chinese takeout. But the best part was still to come; the real part. He could feel the rumblings in his gut as his body chemistry lurched into motion, a highly efficient machine running on the most potent yet refined fuel available.

Frank bought a fresh T-shirt from a street vendor, leaving his own torn jersey on top of an overflowing wire trash basket. *Malcolm X Lives*, the shirt claimed. The dead prophet's silk-screened expression made it look as if he were in on Frank's joke.

He then grabbed a bus Uptown, riding along Lexington Avenue at an excruciatingly slow pace, trapped by mid-afternoon traffic. He enjoyed the early fall sunlight gently warming his face, the toasty belch of automotive exhaust drifting in through his barely open window, the brilliant burst of colours and light made richer by the pale scratched glass of the window, and by the running of the blood that always followed a Feeding, that came shortly before The Passage. Towards the end of the ride, he was a little worried if he'd make it in time. Imagine if it happened here on the orange plastic bus seat, next to a wizened Social Security addict?

When he got to the door of his studio apartment, Frank paused a moment, key in the lock, as he was overwhelmed by the full force of the running. The hallway seemed to quiver, the green wall of mailboxes inhaling and exhaling, the splintered doorjambs dancing. A low machine hum embraced him; it was the sound of his body, working at maximum efficiency. He smiled and let himself in the apartment, unbuttoning his shirt as he went.

Standing nude in the centre of his mostly empty, square-shaped studio space, his chubby body drawn taut so that every muscle sang and rippled on the edge of pain, Frank closed his hands into tight fists, squeezing until nails broke flesh and blue blood welled up in his palms. His little potbelly jumped and quivered with the jolt of pain.

A few drops of blood fell from his right hand, hit the bare but varnished floor, where they jumped as if in protest before sizzling away into nothingness. He lifted the hand to his mouth, superextending his fat, lolling tongue to catch every droplet... licking the joints, the heel of the palm, everywhere. He murmured endearments to his spilled blood.

It was time for The Passage. Lurching past the taped-up photos of bound teenage boys that decorated the inside of his bathroom door, he collapsed into the grime-streaked tub, where psychedelic whorls of green and red mould grew outwards from the corners where porcelain met tile wall. A nearly transparent silverfish darted away across the tile floor, disappearing somewhere underneath the sink.

He began to masturbate, his eyes roving across the Polaroids on the bathroom door, reliving each moment. The pearly grey marrow, the bleached overexposure of the bone shards, the thick, deep crimson in dull streaks and spatters, in flat pools. His boys.

As orgasm approached like footsteps echoing down a distant hallway, The Passage, the final digestion process of The Fee-

ding, approached. Frank's bones began to soften, and his flesh
to run. Waves of peace began to ripple through every atom of
his increasingly liquid form; as he approached a jellied state,
his fingers fused to his cock, and the separate limbs became
one throbbing, undulating mass.

When his climax reached his peak he nearly overflowed the
bathtub with his purer form. The surly young panther's life
essence sparked like St. Elmo's fire layers deep within Frank's
translucent mass, a lightning storm that jerkily faded into
shadowy nothingness. The Feeding was complete.

Club Edelweiss was chaos. It was a warm evening, and an
entire Friday night's worth of transvestite hustlers and their
all-too-eager victims were jammed shoulder-to-falsie at the
long bar facing the disco floor, where the various patrons
stood surveying the lay of the land, hunters and gatherers
come seeking their fortunes.

Only a diminutive Asian transsexual actually danced, lazily
swaying her red leather-clad ass to a Cuban beat. She slowly
moved in a tight circle, flipping her shoulder-length light
brown hair as she went. Her face was young and uncreased,
cheekbones high, eyes black and impenetrable even though
they sparkled with a professional veneer of interest.

Frank observed her avidly from his place at the bar. He
ignored the Brazilian TV next to him, a pretty boy with long
straight black hair and even features, clad in a dark skirt that
reached down to his booted ankles.

"Hey there, Frankie, I think you want some Korean takeout tonight, eh?"

He now looked over at Carmen, who, despite his beauty,
he'd never been moved to take. He'd had him, yes, in that

mundane sense, several times now. It had been satisfying enough, creating that faint sense of friction that humans have to content themselves with.

But something stopped Frank from consuming Carmen, from feeding on his most precious essence. Something maudlin, perhaps: He looked at the mascara-laden young hustler very nearly as a friend. Carmen's brittle jokes and contempt for humanity were tragically sweet, considering his own lowly station — a whore living on hustled White Russians and neatly folded twenties.

"Well, to tell you the absolute truth, Carmen, I was thinking of it, yes indeed. Not to insult your own undeniable charms."

"I'm sure not," Carmen said airily. He was in enough demand, and he knew that most of these tricks were total sluts anyway, ready to suck or be sucked by the next pretty face that drifted by, whether in an expensive fetish dress or just a tight pair of jeans. You took care of yourself, because none of them could be depended on to really love and take care of you.

Frank nodded politely, a half-grin playing about his lips that said he might be back, anyway, if he got shot down. *None of them. Not even Frank*, Carmen thought.

The Asian didn't speak English very well. Trying to communicate with her over the constant clamour of the retro-seventies disco mix was seriously frustrating.

He was finally reduced to a near-hoarse "May I buy you a drink?" that he aided with a little push from his alien will. Though he had the power to tempt souls through the black psychic emanations native to his kind, he preferred to hunt bare-handed, as it were. Drugging a lamb before the slaughter deprives you of the entire melodrama: Those tiny intimations of fear, the sweaty desperation that comes with dawning realisation and finally, that dreamy acceptance and fade-out.

The real art — the real joy — came with a slow, full-scale

seduction. It was what Frank existed to wait for.

Sometimes he wondered about those mortals who shared the same raw soul hunger, the murderers who so fascinated the media, whose exploits filled the newspapers and were splattered across the TV screen. To kill and not feed? What sort of empty, ritualistic masochism was that? Maybe these killers were genetic misfits, the next step in the evolutionary process up to his own long-lived kind. Maybe one had to have the hunger before being able to develop the means to fill it. Or was he just being generous?

The Asian leaned her head lightly against Frank's arm at the bar, her forehead barely reaching his shoulder. She smiled, her teeth strikingly white, made even more so by the diluted touch of the fluorescent bulbs which burned behind the mirrored back wall, where a cheap but plentiful supply of the hard stuff was stacked in glittering pyramids.

"You nice man," she said as if it were a statement, but he knew it was a question.

"I'm a nice man, my friends tell me. Or at least they would, if I had any."

"You friends with Carmen, no?"

"Oh," he smiled, "Carmen is a very dear friend."

"I can be good friend, too."

"I'm sure you will be. What's your name?"

"Ken Su." Her tiny hand found his, fondling the black hairs crisscrossing the pale flesh on its bony back.

Ten minutes later, under Carmen's mocking masquerade of a jealous glare, they were leaving the club, arm in arm. Outside they stood together, Ken Su on the curb and Frank Breedlove in the gutter, waiting to hail a cab. Standing this way, her face was just a few inches below his. Her forehead was directly in line with her lips. He kissed her lightly, there, and mussed her hair. She looked up at him with calculating eyes.

The black waters of the Hudson River danced for them from just across the street. Frank thought he might do this one the really slow way, the old way, and drain her of her blood first. She smiled at him shyly, and it was such an expert feint, he almost felt fooled.

The hotel room was furnished in late cartoon sex-dive; a cheesy vinyl interpretation of glamour, with a Mylar sheet on the ceiling trying to pass for a glass mirror. Putting up the forty dollars for the room had made Frank a generous good-time fella in Ken Su's estimation, however.

But now the bone beneath Ken Su's skin was beckoning him, teasing with its stalwart hardness under the rubbery, easily split cushion of her flesh. He loved the extremely sharp, elegant features of her face, and swooned imagining the beauty of the skull beneath them. A skull like that you might keep, if you were a sentimentalist. Which, Frank had to admit, was a status he could not entirely disavow.

There were the Polaroids back at home, of course, and stuffed into the bottom dresser drawer was a Macy's gift box filled with a pair of grey jockey shorts from the Columbus Circle college kid, charming brat that he'd been. Also a napkin from the Popeye's near Times Square that was discoloured with grease wiped from the lips of the nervous Puerto Rican kid from in front of Port Authority, plus several other piquant *momentos d'amour.*

Ken Su was making small bird noises in her throat, writhing under Frank's grip. His left hand was against the back of her head, the other buried in her ass, two fingers busy relaxing the tissue of her sphincter. With her legs spread out, Frank could watch his knuckle graze her small, hairless testicles, which brushed against the bedspread in a coy manner he found infinitely endearing.

Frank's cock was thick and straight, poking out of his unzipped trousers, worked past the threadbare boxers. Sometimes friction *was* wonderful foreplay, a tempting horduerve before the meal. Ken Su's spare ass was angled up in a feminine curve which demanded he give it one good, hard slap. She burped out a light shriek when he did so, a shriek that degenerated into a fit of hysterical giggles a moment later.

"Ouch, Frank! I thought you nice guy!"

"Nice enough. I was just teasing, sweetie."

"I know that, Frank," she said, drawling out his name in one long, dreamy syllable, the accent making the delivery both alien and child-like. His fingers worked gently in her ass, as a result of which her eyes were hooded with a layer of genuine excitement. Even if it was still glazed over with a constant professional assessment of the work situation.

He fucked her for as long as it amused him, scrutinising the process in a pornographic sort of way. Then he faked an orgasm inside her — that sort of physical function had died somewhere in his distant, dim past — and quickly disposed of the condom before she could see that it was empty.

They were laying together for five minutes, listening to the random street noise, when he felt her tense up, ready to make her move for the bathroom, to clean up and excuse herself and head back to the club in hopes of catching another john or maybe just closing the bar with the small circle of friends she'd made since the long, unpleasant journey from Korea.

Frank was on her gently but swiftly. His hands held her ready, her head forced back and her neck soft and straining, begging to be punctured. He thought of the crude, inviting beer inside her veins and felt his gums swell, the eyeteeth grind against their neighbours as they grew. How long since he'd fed this way? At least a quarter-century.

Her flesh was malleable against the unforgiving hardness of his fangs. Just a moment's studied violence, and it gave way. As the skin split, a frenzy grew within him that his reason could observe with rapt fascination. He felt like a savage in the forest, feasting like this, while the body was still warm and thrashing. A romantic sex-devil conjured around village fires at night to scare the young men and women of the tribe into not straying out into the dark ring of trees, where fates worse than primitive social indiscretion awaited.

He thought he had been that devil, once. He knew he had been many things, over the centuries, though as more and more years rolled by he had trouble remembering the details.

It was odd, once again putting physical effort into the parting of her flesh. Odd but invigorating. When the blood began to jet out into his open mouth, splashing against the back of his palate in a hot, intimate stream, Frank felt his penis re-stiffen, and the hairs on the back of his hand prickle. Her gasps swallowed by the blood flooding her trachea, she beat her small fists against his back, and each blow was a heady massage that increased his pleasure.

Just when he thought it was going to take a very long time yet for her to die, she gave it up. When her life came out of her, sucked rather than free-flowing, he felt warm explosions deep inside him, a boiling cream of sweet napalm. The transfusion of her lifeforce's more vulgarly chemical origins left a metallic aftertaste in his sinuses, behind his eyes, and a slight ringing in his ears. He thought a human would have called it getting drunk, maybe.

He rose from the bed. The crumpled and twisted red polysilk spread beneath her looked, appropriately enough, like a coffin's lining. Ken Su's slightly open mouth, still and undisturbed by any further breeze from her lungs, signalled him it was time to clear his senses, to get his head about him and dispose of the body.

As light as she was, he lurched under her weight when he carried her to the small bathroom and dumped her on the toilet, where he could watch from the tub as she collapsed in on herself, like they all did, no matter how he fed. He clambered into the tub, which had built-in water jets in its sides. He laughed. Drunk, still. It was nice. Frank felt out of control and exultant.

When he left the hotel he walked back past Club Edelweiss, on a forced march through the still, predawn darkness, needing to work off the excess energy that surged through him after The Passage. For some reason, he wanted to sleep through the day, today, and hide inside until it was night again. The very thought of the daylight violating his sallow flesh inspired a dull ache somewhere right behind his eyes.

Night. He'd come out again then, into the noise and chaos of the jungle. Looking for the youngest, most foolish members of the tribe. But first, he'd take Carmen to that diner right next door to Edelweiss, and buy the sweet little Brazilian boy a hamburger, while they made the same old jokes about the girls, the boys, each other, the way the world after all indeed was.

Then Frank Breedlove would excuse himself, and go fill his empty belly.

III

On the tenth day of a sabbatical from the dungeon that both she and The Manager had thought an eminently wise idea, Mary Ellen found herself trapped by her own aimlessness. Her only diversion from the long, eventless hours spent in the apartment were occasional bouts of dread that sent her out to the street, to anywhere where there were other people, no matter how stupid or unpleasant.

Late one such afternoon she found herself heading down Lower Broadway toward Houston, somehow possessed by urgency at the sight of the sky soaking to a deeper blue with every passing minute.

With that orb's retreat, the urban winter's wind sawed away more deeply, raking her cheeks numb, hungrily passing over her bundled curves, seeking to insinuate itself between fabric and flesh. New Year's Eve had heralded several inches of snow, and Manhattan was a shivery vista of grey ice and collapsed white drifts treacherous to navigate, hemming pedestrians together, wet shoulders brusquely struggling past one another, deflecting umbrellas and backpacks.

The insipid neon storefronts of the clothing boutiques and fast-food joints that catered to the tourist and student crowd threw their pink and green radiation across Mary Ellen's face. She felt as safe as a ghost, intangible in the half-light. The light in the dungeon had been so bright and merciless; since then she had found the most peace of mind behind half-drawn shades, by candlelight, just outside of a street lamp's vaporous blaze.

The lighting in the bars she had visited was also bearable, but the glittering array on the back shelves tempted her too mightily, trying to catch her gaze and hypnotise her into submitting to insensibility. Thinking about her life before, Mary Ellen knew that there had already been too much insensibility, too many false havens, chemical or sensual.

It had been ten days since Mary Ellen Masters had woken up to her new world.

Ten days since she had woken up, hands bandaged, to the odd sight of The Manager and his bodyguard and his girl-friend all hovering above, their gazes marked by varying degrees of concern.

Jenny, an alcoholic jazz singer The Manager dutifully supported despite her various incursions against his patience and self-respect, was still holding gauze and surgical scissors. The first-aid tools were actually stocked at the dungeon for use in medical bondage scenes, but now had regained their original purpose during this emergency.

Her thin lips were pursed, her brown eyes forthright with a hard-edged, glinting but still human concern. Mary Ellen stared stupidly at the brown mole situated at the crease of Jenny's mouth; it seemed more vivid, more off-putting, than it ever had before. A dry, cracked plain, like the moon.

Stubby was another matter; her first sight of his face had made her gasp and start, and imagine for a moment she had been drawn back into what she was already starting to think of as The Event. The bodyguard's expression was more primitive than she had ever seen it, his brutal features drawn with feral exaggeration before the menace of this primal miracle: the stigmata that as she walked down the dusky street still itched and burned at the centre of her palms, as the cold wind chapped her white knuckles.

The perfect white saucers of his eyes had seemed to stand out an inch from the ashen details of his dark pelt. His nose twitched frantically with dread, diesel-fuelled by the constant pinches of cocaine he had spent the last three hours loading up on.

The Manager, however, was stone faced, except for his mournful eyes. Mary Ellen was frightened the most by her employer's expression. He was the sort always careful never to show any actual vulnerability except as a managerial tool, a device for better manipulation of the few sweeter-natured girls. Now his eyes were sad as a martyr's, their drooping anguish reflected in the blurry details of Mary Ellen reflected twice over. The ceiling was a hundred miles above the spikes of his stark white hair.

Indeed, the room seemed huge, and somehow displaced, as if it were...somewhere else. She wondered how it was outside the dungeon, if the entire world might have suddenly stumbled one step out of synch with the reality she'd known. In her fear and sick excitement, she felt newly alive.

She thought immediately that it felt like she was waking into a new life, someone else's life. This *was* waking into a new life, even if the physical details were unaltered.

Since Christmas Eve, she had realised that a layer of her skin seemed to have been meticulously sheared away. The low-level interference of static electricity in the air; the cold touch of metal, whether doorknob, fork or coin, were complex, information-filled shocks to her system. She felt exquisitely vulnerable, as well as bereft of whatever naiveté she had spent most of her life uncomfortably cloaked within.

The answering machine filled itself up once every three hours or so, aural proof of the discarded wax of the cocoon she had burst forth from. Friends, ex-lovers, clients, all concerned, having heard second or fourth-hand rumours of Mistress Medusa's sudden, inexplicable breakdown on Christmas Eve. Nobody mentioned her hands, or the blood — maybe The Manager thought it would be bad word of mouth for his business to admit to something so genuinely disturbing and inexplicable.

Even Mary Ellen herself hadn't realised about them, at first; when they started bleeding right before she had fainted she had thought they were part of the harrowing series of hallucinations she had experienced.

But Jenny had wrapped her hands while she was unconscious. She had held the clumsy flippers out before her and seen the sickly gold-copper spots soaking through the gauze, felt the throbbing ache in her palms, one beat off from the drum of her heart.

She'd brushed off the stoned, nervous ministrations of the hushed crew around her, singling out Billy, who looked on the verge of tears as he milled about in the dungeon's doorway, where The Manager had no doubt banished him so he would be out of the way of their first-aid attempts.

"Get me the fuck out of here," she said quietly to him, after she'd shouldered her way past her unusually silent employer.

She reached out to squeeze Billy's big, callused hand. It made her own palm ache more, but she welcomed the slight pain. It sharpened her concentration, and she began to feel, if certainly not back to normal, as if her centre of gravity might at least be within reach again. Like after you vomited during an over-the-top drunk, and regained some of your equilibrium.

Billy instinctively drew back at the dry touch of the bandages, then ducked his eyes from her in guilt.

"Don't worry. It looks worse than it is. Could you just drive me home, please?"

On the street and standing before Billy's Honda, Mary Ellen tasted the sharp, dark air deep in her sinuses. Looking around, she saw that all the buildings on the street, one zoned for light industry, seemed strikingly inert, as if they were all solid inside, with no circulatory systems of hallways and rooms; constructed instead out of building blocks.

Now it felt more like an acid flashback.

Billy fidgeted, holding open the passenger's side door for her. It was still the early hours of Christmas, she'd abruptly remembered, and rested the tip of her chin against the cool window glass for a moment before ducking down inside. A day of miracles.

Now, with ten days contemplation of that day of miracles behind her, ten matching sets of night terrors and long unfocused afternoons, she walked through the freezing heart of January, her feet so cold they now seemed to be made of the concrete under them.

She watched the traffic light change, the stream of cabs and out-of-town license plates gingerly jockey past a stalled neighbour, a jerky stop and go ballet on the ice-covered asphalt.

In the spaces between drifts on the opposite sidewalk, bundled figures ant-crawled at a more steady pace.

A typical winter's day in lower Manhattan. Except it was all different than it had ever been before. Or at least the way she was seeing it was.

Every perception was accompanied by a shifting and a settling, as if the neuron input of the sensory data around her was burning new pathways into a virgin nervous system. As if she'd never seen a traffic light before. Or snow. Even though she knew previous memories of both, as immutably constant symbols, as experiences encountered hundreds of times since childhood, they now signified with a blazing freshness, full of subtle energy playing across their respective surfaces in a jumpy gambol that moved so fast it made a vibrating patina, which translated in soft, shushing whispers detectable only at the very edge of her awareness.

Mary Ellen realised night had fallen, and with that recognition now felt as if the sidewalk were rising up beneath her, but she stood firm, riding its crest as the sky rushed down to meet her and kiss her cheeks, hard sharp night air dirty around the edges with car exhaust, dogfarts, body odour, baking bread, lit matches, spilled blood, Chinese food, wet wool, marijuana. Her limbs felt covered in soft cream as her head began to loll and juices sloshed against the inside of her skull in lopsided circles.

Now it was a mountain she stood upon and the city lay before her was a sparse village, a chimney-smoke hamlet of antiquity, a struggling fire against the cold indifference of nature, and the keen culinary interests of the baser beasts.

It was all simple now: She saw where nature and man met, and where beasts roamed the periphery. Familiar beasts; rapists, child molesters, murderers, confidence men, crackheads, gang-bangers. She'd encountered all these creatures before, either in the flesh or through the ever-unsettling influence of television and the papers. Yes, a few of them, she certainly knew much too well, as she now finally had come to realise; a memory of her father, his hands finally stilled on the day of his funeral, came to her.

The thought of her father made the vision abruptly recede, but before completely faded she caught a glimpse of something else, a different sort of beast. Several types, in fact, exotic and deadly, taunting with some primal familiarity before retreating into the misshapen anonymity of totally alien miens.

Then she was back on the sidewalk, the sidewalk back on the earth, and she nearly lost her balance as an impatient businessman jolted her shoulder on his determined way past, practically jostling her off the curb and into the slush.

Lions and tigers, oh my, she thought crazily. Gravity taunting her, she looked around for a fast food restaurant or diner where she could sit down before she fainted.

The pink and white gleam of a Dunkin Donuts welcomed her, so clean and safe, so shiny and smooth…her thoughts tried to deliberately disassociate as she sat at the counter, already instinctively trying to recreate the vanished rapture. But the chrome gleam of the counter was too distracting, too strangely sensuous.

It was back to a low level hum now, that electric crackle, initially so alien and now after her vision almost a welcome friend.

"Yes, may I help you, please?" A short Indian woman asked her, her utterly professional cheerfulness not doing a good job of masking her near-terror at Mary Ellen's dreamy, seemingly drug-induced state. Mary Ellen could read her thoughts: *Not another junkie with a bandaged handful of dimes and pennies.*

"Coffee with. No sugar. A bran muffin," she ordered by rote, relying on uninterrupted years of bad dietary habits to carry her through this act of normalcy. The counter girl moved away warily after serving her, relieved to serve the next customer, a balding fat man in a rumpled business suit.

Mary Ellen stared at the woman, and saw through her skin. Saw the capillaries, the layers of fat, the bone, gristle and blood. Like an exploded cutaway view, the vision sprung upon her, startling her into slopping the hot coffee all over the saucer, light brown drops dappling the Formica beyond.

The woman looked toward her and frowned even as she

plucked a vanilla-frosted cruller from the crumb-strewn wax-papered tray. Oddly, her absurdly sudden mutilation seemed to phase her not at all, despite the gruesome wet pulsing of organ, the white gleam of bone, the dull ripple of fat, the fishy pulse of eyeball.

Mary Ellen shut her eyes and put her hands to her temples and massaged, pressing hard enough to send green and gold rings surging up out of the blackness. She let the luminous impressions of her corneas projected onto the empty screens of flesh distract her, soothe her. Hypnotised by the flashing light. Nothing there but the light. The light was safe.

When she opened her eyes the counter girl was whole again, brown skin and pink and white standard-issue uniform in place. She was handing the fat man his change, careful to drop the coins in his palm without touching him. He looked disappointed as he swung the plastic sack with box of a dozen assorted off the counter. Mary Ellen wondered if he was going to eat them all himself.

"Do you need anything else?" the counter girl asked, trying to prompt Mary Ellen to move along. Avoiding the girl's dark glare, she left the coffee and muffin sitting on the counter and hiked back to her apartment.

IV

A neatly parked row of customised Harleys, each unique-
ly styled, all polished to perfection, crowded the curb in
front of the clubhouse. The setting sun bounced off a
silver fender at a long, low angle that kissed the asphalt nearly
to the other side of the street. The welcome quiet on this block
of the East Village was almost unnatural in its rarity.

Though there were a few brittle yuppies in the freshly-con-
verted condo two doors down who were nervous on typical-
ly general yuppie principal about sharing the street with the
Reivers, the block's long-time residents tended to be grateful
for the protection.

True, there were the occasional thunderous symphonies on
the odd early morning that saw the launching of a platoon of
brothers on a cross-country ride. But the block was miracu-
lously free of drug dealers, peace punks or belligerent homeless; no mean feat in the East Village, where you couldn't walk
half a block down most streets without being panhandled,

mugged or offered bad drugs.

One of the club's prospects held watch in front of the unassuming old tenement that some twenty years ago had been painted black, fortified and converted into the Reivers' headquarters.

His arms were folded over his chest, half hiding the plain breast of his denim vest, still awaiting patches and badges he hadn't yet earned the right to display. He was small but those arms looked like carved pine. He peered at Mary Ellen from behind smoky grey Wayfarers as she approached. She knew he wouldn't bother to speak until he was addressed. Watch was watch, after all. Once he was a full brother there would be pussy and world enough.

"Here for Axel," she informed him, skipping the greeting and defensively resting her fists on her soft hips, which she cocked toward the sky as if to say *I've fucked better than you into unconsciousness*.

"He expecting you?"

She sniffed the air, wondering if the brothers had taken the required group leak on him yet. His vest was clean and stiff; his grin callow and arrogant; she decided that pleasure still lay before him.

"Yeah. Tell him Mary Ellen's here."

The prospect ambled inside, slamming the reinforced steel door firmly shut behind him, just in case Mary Ellen made a run for it, and invaded the clubhouse. God knows what would happen, then! How tiresome machismo could become.

Two minutes later, though, Mary Ellen's mood changed abruptly at the sight of Axel peeping out of that same door, his long, chestnut-hued hair damp and dark from a fresh shower.

Her irritation dissipated when he fixed her with a friendly gaze of surprise and cracked a familiar warm grin that made Mary Ellen feel slightly limp with relief.

"Mary Ellen! What, you felt like slummin' today?"

She rolled her eyes, and fought down the expected stirrings of desire Axel raised in her. She had dated a brother once, for a time, and when that draining, near-violent relationship was over, she had declared herself through with bikers. She now looked upon Axel, who never treated her with anything less than forthright respect and quiet support, as the right choice she didn't make when she had the chance.

"They said at the bar you'd probably be here."

"Oh, them boys at the bar. Checkin' up on me, eh? Well, hey, come on up," he invited, one hard-muscled arm swinging the heavy door all the way open to allow Mary Ellen in. Her hips visibly switched back and forth under her long black coat, as she pointedly ignored the prospect who waited stiff-necked and impatient to take up his sentry post again.

Axel didn't bother speaking as he vaulted up the long narrow steps. Mary Ellen followed close, provoked by the way the t-shirt he had obviously just thrown on after his shower stuck to the wet spots on his broad, muscular back. She loved his unassuming but formidable air of masculinity; the chance to be near it kept her only a couple of steps behind him up all three of the clubhouse's lopsided, twisting staircases.

After securing an iron bar across the front door of his small, neat apartment in the back of the building, he gestured for her to sit.

"Grab some couch, whydoncha. Want some tea or somethin'? Fresh outta crumpets."

She would have liked a beer, actually. But Axel, though he made most of his living as a bouncer at various beer and whiskey dives around the city, didn't drink. You never saw him fucked up on anything, in fact, though he wasn't AA or anything.

"Tea would be great," Mary Ellen agreed as she settled onto the red, plush Victorian couch and braced her boot heels against one of the brass handles on the chestnut coffin Axel had turned into a coffee table. Slots for the glass top were welded into each corner, under the dust-free glass you could see the skeleton from a medical supply house that occupied the velvet interior.

Axel set the water boiling on an antique but immaculately-kept gas stove before going to a long bookshelf filled with oversize red binders, each with its own neatly lettered label on the spine.

Selecting one, he tossed it on her lap and knelt before her, gesturing for her to look.

She smiled, grateful for the distraction from her nightmares and brooding over her Christmas Eve client and the disturbingly vivid, seemingly revelatory hallucinations that had been following her since soon after.

The photos in the album were of Axel's display table at the last Long Island rally he'd attended. Spread out on black velour was his entire line of fancifully-designed knives and historically accurate daggers, sword canes with intricately carved handles; even a great broadsword of such brute beauty it would have made Arnold Schwarzenegger drool.

"Wow," Mary Ellen said, tongue-tied. Axel poured his rough-cornered soul into his work, and to anyone but a critic, his soul was indeed on intimate terms with whatever muses heralded beauty and majesty. The daggers looked as though they should be adorning the waists of long-bearded Celtic kings during ceremonies of office. If only there were kings left to wear them.

"This one's really amazing," Mary Ellen said, pointing to a snapshot of a simple but elegant design, a dagger with a dragon's fanged mouth for a pommel, spread wings forming the finger guard.

"Yeah, that one came out pretty good, after a couple of

months work," Axel allowed, handing over her cup of tea before fetching that very blade from the shelf for her to examine. It was a foot long overall, and quite heavy in her hand.

"Iron," he explained, grinning. "You don't even have to stick anybody with it. You can just whack them over the head."

She ran her fingers down its length, and a moment later was embarrassed by the obvious sexuality of her gesture. Axel, however, had either not noticed or politely pretended he hadn't.

"So how's shit goin' up at the dungeon? You gettin' along with The Manager?" he questioned, plopping down next to her on the sofa, albeit a safe six inches away. Why was she feeling so randy all of a sudden?

"The usual trash, and more," she told him. "It's a living. Maybe a little weirder than usual, lately."

Axel let the statement lay there; his code of chivalry was such that he wouldn't question a female friend on her sexual habits, not even if they were a professional matter. After a moment, Mary Ellen went on, anyway.

"I had a really crazy experience on Christmas Eve, though. It kind of left me looking at the world in a whole different way," she continued.

That was an innocent enough way to ease him into it. Sitting next to him, breathing in the soap-tinged odour of his freshly bathed skin, watching the muscles move under his arms, Mary Ellen became aware that a drop of lubrication was squeezing out between her legs.

Her excitement increased the acuteness of her newest sense; her vision seemed to sharpen, as objects around her stood out more clearly; the brass joints of the coffin shone nearly bright enough to make her squint.

She could also smell vividly the old sex in the air, differentiate between the different odours: of Axel's come, of several different female spoors.

Jealous, she wondered who Axel had fucked here last. Some biker groupie, no doubt, one of the tough-talking, slutty bunch who faithfully attended every Reivers party. Some of them aspired to be Old Ladies; others were just cock-hungry, and often ended up drunk and pulling a train of at least five or six brothers.

Mary Ellen had gotten drunk at several Reivers parties, but Axel had always been there to look out for her, never taking advantage of her himself even when she nearly cried out in frustration for him to do just that.

"So how's the dildo business," she asked him. Working the register at a Times Square adult bookstore was another of Axel's several odd jobs besides the bouncer gigs. Exquisite as the blades he designed were, they had yet to start turning enough of a profit to keep his chopped '71 Sportster and '47 Plymouth in proper repair and high gloss.

"It's on the rise, or so they tell me," he cracked. "Different faces everyday, same bunch of sick motherfuckers. Moving lots of the extra-longs lately; I hear Mother's Day's coming."

She giggled in spite of herself, and ached for him to be closer; even from here her skin tingled from the kiss of his aura, a pulse of moral strength and physical confidence. It made her feel safe; she wanted him to take her in his arms, so she could pretend Christmas Eve had never happened.

Instead, she kept trying to explain things to him.

"Seriously though, Axel, things have been kind of disturbing, lately."

"Oh yeah," he answered, warily, suspecting she might want to get what he would call "all female" on him. Axel was great at solving all sorts of problems, but he didn't have the taste for emotional melodrama of any sort.

"There was this weird guy who came into work on Christmas Eve, and things happened... things I can't really explain, that I don't really understand, and since then I haven't felt really... safe," she stuttered, sounding vague but urgent.

"Well, you got my beeper number, Mary Ellen," Axel said, spinning the sleek iron knife between his left palm and right fingertip in a meaningful gesture.

"I appreciate that," she replied, feeling only a little reassured. He couldn't do anything about it if he didn't know what it was, and she knew he'd never believe her.

"Don't worry about it, Mary Ellen. Anybody screws with you, me and a couple of the fellas will be only too happy to introduce the sucker's face to the asphalt and his bones to a tire iron," Axel assured her. He was not boastful by nature, obviously, though, he could see the need for some strong reassurances for the nearly trembling woman sitting next to him.

Fuck! How could she ever hope to explain her new reality to him? Did she even have to, or were they both better off if she just let him think some pervert was stalking her?

How could she ever make him believe the real problem? *Hey, Axel, I've been the victim of a weird supernatural manifestation that raped me with the power of unwanted knowledge, leaving me flayed and vulnerable to the fear of the black things that now keep lurking at the periphery of my vision?*

She didn't need her new, improved powers of perception to see that Axel would tell her she'd been watching too many schlocky horror movies and suggest a long, soothing vacation.

"Hey, want to go get a beer at Seven Seventeen?" Axel asked, unfolding his legs and rising from the sofa.

"Sure, great," Mary Ellen chirped, trying to keep down a note of disappointment. This wasn't turning out at all the way she had hoped. She had worked herself up to thinking that Axel, smart, practical, strong Axel, might understand, if only she could explain it to him correctly.

But she couldn't. She couldn't tell anyone, not him, not

Billy, certainly not The Manager. Gathering her purse and coat, she prepared to depart Axel's reassuring, heavily fortified little domain. She felt a burst of self-pity that she couldn't come hide here, among the daggers and the tea.

"Hey, wasn't your birthday a few days ago?" Axel suddenly asked, rinsing out the teacups and setting them carefully in a black plastic drainboard.

"A week. Don't remind me how old I'm getting," said Mary Ellen.

"We're all getting old. Here's something to console you in your waning years," Axel teased, as he fetched the dragon blade from the coffee table and pressed it into Mary Ellen's hands.

Making small noises of delight, she turned the gift over in wonderment. Holding this piece of Axel, of his strength and good nature, made her feel immediately better. Admiring the craftsmanship, she saw that he had carved several runes into the blade itself, light and elegant etchings that only became clear when held at an angle to the light.

"Just some stuff from my book collection."

"You're kidding. You want me to have this?"

"Hey, why not? It's the first cast. Collector's item, right? Naw, really. Just somethin' nice between friends. Use it wisely."

She looked up into his blue eyes for a moment, straight through to the simple, clean depths of his soul. Then she buried her face in his shoulder, trying to obscure tears of grief that there was no permanent place of retreat for her in that azure lake. She wondered, as she had many times before, if it had been becoming a professional mistress that had squelched any romance between them.

"So what do the runes *mean*?" she asked him after she had composed herself, and carefully stowed his gift in her oversize leather purse.

"Protection against evil; overcoming obstacles. Thor's hammer is on there; that means you're under the protection of the God of Thunder himself, that big drunken lout."

She giggled, and gave him a peck on the cheek. Anything more would have not been well received.

The prospect was still at his post at curbside. She met his insolent gaze on the way out, and wished she could dump the burden of her knowledge on him. How would a punk like that deal with the ocean of shit rising around her boots? How would anybody? She swung one leg over the back of Axel's bike and wondered if she would find a way, short of madness or suicide.

V
_____

Seven Seventeen was crowded for so early on a winter's evening. A freezing rain during the afternoon had left the East Village streets shiny and treacherous, yet people still stirred out of their burrows, made restless by this year's particularly punishing winter.

The only good thing about the chill was that it kept the crazies and the panhandlers somewhat at bay. Mary Ellen had already learned to dislike the chaotic energy that flowed around them; anguish and anger, despair and schizophrenia. Like unruly bursts of static ruining a radio broadcast, their presence broke up the processing of the data that her fresh sense took in by means of whatever ghost organ it was she had grown; that semi-benign tumour which when it stirred felt part magnetic and part a thing made from the ether.

And in such moments of distraction and confusion, disoriented by the madness rocketing inside the head of some human refuse, Mary Ellen would float there in the blank band, denatured of all logical thought process, and sense The Threat loud and clear, just like she had on that twilight stroll down Broadway.

Here in the bar, however, sitting next to Axel, cushioned by the familiar bluster of several already drunk bikers on either side of them, she felt secure.

She was on her version of Holy Ground; in the old days, when she had been much more frisky, some of her best one-nighters had been born here. That American Indian boy with the smooth black hair down to his waist; what a delicious cock he had owned. She felt a sudden ache to know what Axel's cock looked like. Two of her fingers stroked the birthday gift he had just given her through her purse, the iron blade seeming to radiate coolness up through the leather. She imagined using her mouth making his cock that hard.

Her peaceful, horny rapture soon dissolved, however. They had been sitting at the front bar only a short time, not even through their first round, when Mary Ellen began to feel inexplicably tense and uncomfortable, the pit of her stomach rumbling with an unexplained urgency.

She made another attempt to explain The Event to Axel; it went about as well as she had feared it would.

"So what you're tellin' me here, is that you had an acid flashback on Christmas Eve while you workin', and it really freaked you out," Axel said.

"No, *like* an acid flashback. But crazy as it sounds, real," she repeated.

Axel nodded his head in a gravely paternal manner so silly it almost dissipated her frustration. But not quite. Taking a pull from the tiny red and white bar straw floating at the top of his coke, he began what she feared would be an extremely polite and well-meaning but patronising mental-health commercial suggesting a vacation from the whips and tips business; time to get off the stiletto heels for awhile, perhaps.

"You're a very sensible young lady, I think you know that. But your line of work is kinda difficult for even the most together chick, if you know what I mean — "

She wanted to rap her knuckles against the bar top to subsume her frustration with a little physical pain. Instead she repressed her anger so fiercely it came out as a whine that was grating even to her own ears.

"Ax-UL! I have not lost my mind over this stupid business! I know the difference between fantasy and reality, unlike all those people who buy your swords and run around pretending they're Conan the Barbarian!"

Axel looked hurt for a moment, his veneer of macho inscrutability yanked out of place. Mary Ellen felt terribly guilty. She turned her head away in embarrassment. And gasped in fright.

There was something in the back room of Seven Seventeen that simply could not exist. A dragon. A fucking dragon, right out of a fairy tale.

She gaped at this latest hallucination, her skin crawling just as it had in Dungeon One on Christmas Eve. The bar room felt similarly volatile and charged, though with a more menacing, predatory current. She knew immediately that the thing she was looking at, for all its ancient power, was a gross, savage threat. And she was fascinated.

When the dragon breathed, the scales on its throat rippled, shiny grey-emerald. Coiled awkwardly on a bench back by the jukebox, it flexed serpentine muscles beneath iridescent skin in spastic restlessness. The flat head ducked toward the table as it surveyed the bar with golden orbs split vertically by black pupils. Nictitating membranes rode across the eyeballs' curves with lazy regularity, jostled into a more hurried repetition the nearer the head swung towards the brighter parts of the room.

Then, all its limbs — how many were there, exactly? — seemed to whip against each other in a moment's frenzy, at the very instant its inhuman head settled its gaze in her direction. Those alien eyes stared at Mary Ellen Masters, lit by something that resembled racial hatred, yet was somehow more disturbingly personal.

Attempting to remain calm, Mary Ellen tried to reason how much of a real danger the dragon might present; after all, despite everything she had gone through in Dungeon One, she had remained physically unharmed — except, of course, for the stigmata, which had not been directly caused by any of the visitors.

As if on cue, her palms began to itch in a wickedly insistent manner. She rubbed them against the wet bar top, hoping to ease the discomfort.

Half terrified she was indeed falling victim to some mental illness, Mary Ellen deliberately looked away from the monstrosity, at her half-full gin and tonic. When she looked back, it was still there, still seemingly staring at her.

It was definitely time for a second opinion. After her insult, Axel had politely involved himself in a conversation with the bartender.

"Hey, could you please look over there," Mary Ellen said, tugging at her companion's elbow.

"Orders, orders. Whatever you say, sister."

The biker swung around on his stool and squinted in the direction Mary Ellen had allowed the barest nod. Scratching his unkempt lion's mane, he stared blankly for a moment, then turned to her.

"Look at what? You mean that dumpy old guy suckin' down his social security check?"

She spun back and forth on her own stool, surveying the group of tables in the back room. She saw no dumpy old man. There were a couple of would-be biker sluts, wearing too much eyeliner and flared hip-hugger jeans. And a big, bald-headed black man who looked as serene as Buddha, holding court to two skinny dealer-types. But no dumpy old man.

Axel wasn't seeing what she was; he was in fact seeing what, logically, she imagined she should have been.

Now Mary Ellen thought it seemed quite likely she was insane. The visions and all these new impressions were merely the symptoms of her progressing mental illness. Her head swam and she felt faint; her drink boiled in her suddenly unsettled stomach. Afraid she was going to be sick right at the bar, maybe even on Axel, sweet Axel whom she'd never have, who if she was lucky might come bring her candy on visiting day at the nuthouse, she dismounted her stool.

"Excuse me, I'll be right back," Mary Ellen said, and lurched toward the bathroom, leaving Axel with his mouth hanging open and a furrowed brow.

Frank stared back at the nervous woman with the striking dark hair who had picked him out, his spine prickling with a distantly familiar fear and repulsion. From the violence of the instincts she roused in him, he felt sure he must had somehow met her before, though it seemed impossible that he would forget such an incident.

Though his more ancient memories had indeed faded over the centuries, he could recall the last fifty years perfectly, and a rare, unhappy moment such as being recognised for what he was by a human would still stand out in sharp relief against the predictable, repeated ignorance of all his prey, stalked and consumed in hurried feedings or lazy, drifting hunts.

The food, as a rule, couldn't recognise those who would harvest them. It was not in their nature; they lacked some necessary sense, evidently surviving on only five meagre ones. These days especially, when man imagined he knew the shape of the universe, you could safely walk right up to them, even tell them what you were, and, if they were a level-headed citizen in good standing, they would not doubt for a moment that you were simply one of them who had lost his mind; gone lunatic.

Their vision, their hearing, their smell were all pitifully insufficient, unable to recognise and process the discrete wavelengths of information that marked a Feeder's presence. Their handicapped nature was one of the reasons why Frank had lived so long in this incarnation, safely stalking their desensitised urban veldts.

Still, this woman at the bar recognised him for what he was, he was certain of it. And despite her obvious terror at the sight of him, her blue eyes still flashed with the inbred hatred all competing species have for each other, her mouth was drawn up in horror and disgust.

Making that ridiculous face, she somehow looked more familiar. Was it her features, or her expression? A faint, thoroughly suppressed memory plucked at Frank, something more than a thousand years old.

Water. He had been living in water, at the time. The feeding was easy, then; he had so cowed an enclave of these little pink things that they would gladly procure him his dinners, delivering up a succession of succulent little things not so different from that sweet, fresh Darren, whom he had left three-quarters consumed in the movie theatre's men's room.

Everyone had been younger then, not only their mortal race, but himself as well. In fact, he'd been a stupid and primitive beast who had thought himself lord of the earth's dominion for as far as he could see it stretch, which from his rock there in the middle of the lake really wasn't very far at all. Life had been nothing but pleasure, then, exulting in the fury of his new-born essence, igniting the very oxygen around him with his hardy exhalations, capering down into the warm, loamy bosom of mother earth, sunning himself unafraid under the white orb that kissed the then-verdant planet where he dwelled.

The more he dredged up these memories of his infancy, the clearer it became to him: it was indeed not her face but her expression that was shockingly familiar. He had seen it once before, and once before only.

It had been on that black day that his murderer came calling, rigid and sweating astride a rightfully terrified, snorting horse. Come to steal his life away.

His murderer was a man, but no ordinary man. Armed with lance and sword, the sun glinting off the crest of his iron war helmet, his chest and limbs were covered with a hard, shiny shell, like one of the waterbugs Frank would swallow between meals. On that shell was painted a large red cross.

Frank had been in a particularly vulnerable spot, not in the water but not sequestered in his subterranean nest, either. The metal-covered man had ambushed him there, planting himself between lake and cavern, blocking any possible path of retreat.

Not that retreat had been on Frank's mind; not at first. He had reared back, whipping his many limbs about, large, strong, youthful and bold, not yet wizened to this pseudo-human form he was nowadays cursed with, except during the brief respites of the Passage.

He had spit his venom at the silent challenger, a pale acid that blinded the steed and made the metal of the man's breastplate sizzle and pop loudly in the otherwise still Spring afternoon, and dissolved away most of whatever pigment had been used to draw the cross.

But the man had been unimpressed and unafraid. Quickly dismounting, comforting his rearing mount with a single pat on the muzzle and some whispered words that Frank could not hear from his perch, he drew his sword and stalked forward, demanding engagement.

Frank's fury was nearly overwhelming, though now a new, unpleasant flavour had suddenly been introduced to his otherwise bucolic way of life: Fear. The man's very expression inspired it; the way as he came closer his stare stayed unflinchingly locked into Frank's then-yellow eyes, boring through to the Stygian depths of his wriggling soul.

Cursing his own fear, Frank had thrashed about, his arms and legs in a rebellious panic, as if his tormentor's gaze had somehow ignited some uprising in his very blood.

There was a consuming blaze in the tormentor's clear blue eyes, a blue-white conflagration of tremendous heat and light, too large to have been authored by this small, simple construct of brittle bone and tender flesh. Frank sensed the second-hand presence of Another, one who was the real intruder here, a greater beast or engine boasting a gaping, insistent maw, an insatiable hunger that dwarfed his own mean needs for the small ones of the tribe that served him here in his lakeside domain.

He had come to understand that presence since then, and here, in the bar, he knew It for what It was. Slowly, the woman whom had recognised him was sliding from her barstool, one still hand braced against the scarred lip of the mahogany bar top for purchase.

Her mouth fell slightly open, as if to raise an alarm, and Frank cringed, his knee banging the uneven table and slopping a bit of beer over his hand. Stupidly, he had imagined for a moment that she was going to spit the same blue-white flames at him across the barroom that the murderer had a millennium ago, the flames that had charred his flesh, made him helplessly thrash and howl while the human closed the distance between them to run him through with his crude, iron sword.

It hadn't been the sword that had weakened him so much as the implacable energy that by then was radiating from his attacker's every pore, seeping up through the soft pink flesh and the damaged armour that covered it, attacking Frank's body with piercing rays of light that ran him through so many fold their excruciating paths crossed a hundred times each through his heart, his intestines, shuddering muscles and exploding capillaries.

Only by dragging himself to the edge of the lake and tumbling down into the churning froth of the disturbed waters had Frank barely rescued his existence that black day.

As it was, he had slept for nearly two hundred years after that, his healing an excruciating process as he evolved, finally twisted and reduced to something like the spare, less than graceful creature he now was. No longer majestic, no longer fire-breathing, instead a mere shadow of his glorious youth, cursed to live in this mockery of a form that aped the appearance of the very grubs he fed upon.

That's what they were. Grubs. Worms. The mean fuel of his continued existence. The woman at the bar would be just one such grub, Frank decided, blessed by the same unseen adversary as his murderer or not.

He would consume her before that stricken look of recognition in her eyes could coalesce into something truly threatening. If there was time, maybe he could rape her as well. As he grew closer to the ferocity he had known so many centuries ago, he found the taste for intercourse with these delicate little food things staying with him, even if his attention to any gentle nuance had paled considerably.

But now that he preferred once more to consume his food raw, rather than settle for siphoning off its essence, a couple of tears in the package didn't count for much, in the way of things.

When the agitated woman slid off her seat and headed away from him and toward the rest rooms, he smiled and licked his dry, cracked lips. Already hungry. Drew a circle in the sweat from his beer glass that had leeched onto the tabletop. Then closed his eyes, counted to ten, and rose to follow her.

This was certainly more exciting than stalking those poor, stupid little cows at the transvestite bars, or in the public parks. There was an element of intrigue and danger, what with the way he stood out here; his aspect was not that of one of this particular tribe.

Frank shivered as, in the lower half of his body, sexual excitement and hunger intertwined in heady confusion.

VI

Good lord Jesus save me from that monster, save me from my own madness. She mouthed the words to herself, holding her hands under the stream of cold water, her palms cupped in an aspect of prayer, heart pounding as the cool wetness eased the infernal itching of her palms.

If "Whipping Post" hadn't been blaring so loudly from the jukebox, Mary Ellen could have heard the cracking and splintering of the bathroom door as the steel plate around the knob was ripped from its place.

Thanks to an overload of Duane Allman, however, it was only when the door gave, and the furious slide guitar riffs finally leaked all the way in, that Mary Ellen, distracted by her own panic, sensed the change.

She turned just in time to confront the uncoiled and looming dragon, scales on its neck flared and translucent, dancing with quicksilver colours.

Stumbling back in fright, her gaze was drawn against her

will to the beauty of the surprisingly complex muscles working under the flesh of the long, scarred snout that was suddenly only two feet away from her own face. The noxious gas of the beast's exhalation singed the hairs inside her nostrils and made her eyes water.

Blinking the tears from her eyes, she cast her gaze downward for an instant, and became even more terrified: The dragon bore an elegant, merciless saurian erection, jutting like a spear from between its squat, heavily muscled set of hind legs.

If the monstrosity had appeared just moments earlier, she would have never known the moment of her death; she had been in a place of prayer above the grimy toilet, making an unsuccessful attempt to purge herself of her hallucinations along with the brown rice and sautéed green beans that had made a hurried dinner a few hours earlier.

The purge had not been successful. She was obviously still mad, for here was her illness, coalesced into such vivid form she could hear it, smell it, feel its stifling corporeality straining to embrace and penetrate its creator.

Why not let it? Perhaps that way, the madness might end, disappearing in on itself. Or of course, she might be submerged there forever. But either way would be a resolution.

As the foul creature advanced a slither and began to snuffle at her, the talons at the end of its spidery forelimbs flexed for a strike, and she succumbed to cowardice and shut her eyes. Her fingers tightened spastically around the mouth of her purse.

She started when her thumb scratched against a jagged burr on a corner of the metal clasp holding the bag shut. A brief series of sparks fell across the curtain of her eyelids, a galvanising gift of pain.

And there in the blackness that remained after their passing she finally saw clearly the incredible, terrible truth that had been in front of her this whole time: Mary Ellen Masters was entirely sane and in possession of her faculties. Those senses, rather than failing her, truly had been transformed; the intermittent hallucinations and odd dream states she had gone through since Christmas Eve constituted a difficult awakening to a new, unimaginable level of perception.

Now she knew: There was more to the world than the flesh, and more to the flesh than humankind thought. There were forces that had no need for skin, there were energies with no need for thought, there were changelings and other creatures clothed in skin too slyly mutable to be detected by the sort of blind creature she had until just recently been.

There was The Threat, and it was a not a thing but a place; the place the dragon had come forth from. Dark, endless and hungry. The Black.

Her eyes were still shut, and though she no longer saw the beast, she could smell it, hear it, feel its mass displace the air, even taste the rancid condensation from its breath settling on her tongue. She flinched, ready for her grand revelation to be short-lived.

Improbably, a familiar voice rang over Duane Allman's slide solo.

"Hey Mack! Can I have a moment of your attention, there?"

Mary Ellen's eyes snapped open. Over the prehensile wings jutting from the dragon's back, Axel's face was peering into the bathroom, his gaze locating her, putting her under his protection.

The biker clamped one of his rough, oil-stained hands tightly on the bony ridge of the dragon's shoulder.

"Hey, I think you're in the wrong rest room, buddy," Axel said brusquely, prepared to pull the thing back into the barroom, where he would have room to deal with it. Mary Ellen realised with dismay that Axel could not see the dragon for what it was, and instead thought it a man.

Emitting a long, sibilant hiss, the dragon moved impossibly fast, turning and wrapping one of its sinuous limbs around the biker, lifting him from his feet and pulling him forward into the women's room.

Axel's two hundred pounds hurtled through the air and knocked Mary Ellen sideways. Pain blossomed in her hip from being driven against the cool white sink, which half-collapsed underneath her. The dragon slithered its bulk into the narrow, long cubicle behind them, drawing the door with cracked, ancient talons without even looking back, the music again sealed out.

Axel was only momentarily stunned, however. With a barbarian roar, he was up off the floor and flinging himself without hesitation on his adversary.

The breath hadn't even seeped back into Mary Ellen's constricted chest yet, and she was still blinking away the spots of pain before her eyes: something sharp had stuck her in the thigh.

Axel's hands were shaving scales off the dragon's neck as he scrabbled for purchase around the mighty reptile's throat; his back arched with the mighty effort.

But the dragon appeared unperturbed, rearing its head up as if in laughter or an impending yawn. A new tune had come on the jukebox; it was a loping death-metal anthem, the lyrics in Spanish.

"*Rosa muerte, negro suerte,*" a gravely voice bellowed over guitars that sounded like hammer blows.

"*Motherfucker,*" Axel accused as the gaping, angular snout reached the apex of its loll and fell swiftly back down, engulfing his left shoulder. A moment later, it had been bit into two parts, straight through leather, denim, flesh, muscle and bone.

The dragon's front claws now came around to embrace its suddenly limp enemy, shredding even more leather and denim as treacherous talons clutched and swiped, drawing the meat closer.

Axel weakly tried to beat against the predator's skull with his remaining fist; it responded by swallowing that limb up to the elbow, and biting it off. The resultant spray of gore painted two of the walls and part of the mirror above the sink with long, drooling dashes of red. Mary Ellen felt a few hot drops rebound against her cheek, even from where she was cowering on the opposite side of the room.

Axel's mouth hung open, working silently; the shock was too much for him even to scream. The music continued pounding, prerecorded and oblivious to the violence for which it was providing a sickly appropriate soundtrack. Speared by hopelessness, Mary Ellen stared at her dying friend, and couldn't help but realise that his thrown-back head and twisted features made him look like the Jesus on the cross who had haunted her childhood dreams, inseminated there by an insistent church.

Tossing Axel aside to die, the dragon blew black ether from its nostrils and ambled forward. Playfully slow, gratingly confident. Nictitating orbs fixed in her direction, beckoning for her attention, whispering that they had a message, little morsel, just be quiet and listen... Mary Ellen hated this vile creature more than she had hated anything in her whole life, father included.

Still positive she was going to die, she was seized by a need to at least make her tormentor feel some pain, to leave some rueful scar on its repulsive hide. But how, how, how?

Slumping down the dusty tile wall, stale graffiti ink smeared against her palms, stinging the skinned flesh. They were bleeding again, but this time of natural cause; she had scraped them in the fall.

Tearing away from the dragon's gaze before she could be fully mesmerised, Mary Ellen saw where her purse had fallen.

It was by the filthy base of the toilet, most of its contents scattered. Through a split in the leather poked the tip of Axel's gift, the beautiful, heavy cast iron dagger. She realised that the knife was what had scratched her thigh.

She had nothing to lose.

Now boldly staring the dragon directly in its alien eyes, trying to keep its attention diverted, she felt her way to the purse and twisted open the clasp. She got her hand around the blade; gripping too tightly at first, the edge laid open the pads of two fingers.

The dragon didn't notice her manoeuvre; her nemesis seemed as terribly fascinated by her gaze as she was by its own. She suspected that as long as she kept looking, it would not break away, not until the moment of her murder. She carefully angled the hilt into her fist, gripping extra tightly because the metal was now slippery with her blood.

The dragon continued its advance, and she could see on the lower periphery of her vision that the monster's obscene erection had not only grown but begun to metamorphose, some gelid grey lozenge now sliding up out of the scaly sheath, unleashing an unbelievably raw stink that made her start to gag.

As if insulted by her reaction, the beast sprung forward. She answered the attack with an upward thrust of Axel's dagger.

Teeth gritted, she jabbed upward, and was almost thrown off balance by how easily the blade slid into the creature's chest.

Kicking for purchase against the wet, slimy floor, she hung on desperately as the thing thrashed about, angry and spastic, doing its best to dislodge the offending metal.

Giddy with fear and adrenaline as she was spun about by the dragon's convulsions, Mary Ellen glimpsed the grim tableau made by Axel's languishing, mutilated corpse and made a crazy, quicksilver leap of logic: The blade jammed in the creature's chest had been fashioned by a martyr's hand.

Whatever the reason, the blade certainly seemed to be more effective than she could have hoped against this impossible monster. Its reaction to the intrusion of its flesh by the iron seemed almost allergic; a massive hood now flared around the lizard-thing's three-foot thick neck, and the razor points of two six-inch, discoloured fangs were obscured by great foamy cascades of stinking, crackling drool.

And now the head abruptly ceased its helpless paroxysms, frozen into place in front of the bathroom's rough-edged mirror. The nictitating membranes stopped revolving, and the dragon's black eyeballs began to swiftly dry and pucker. The patina of light from its own reflection speckled the monster's flesh like steaming drops of silvery rain.

Steam rose off the serrated scales, and the creature's former thrashing and writhing gave way to a helpless, frustrated quiver.

The blade fell out, striking the floor with a clatter that over the punishing death metal sounded like a pin striking a pillow.

Or no, it had been pushed out, Mary Ellen saw, by some flex of the makeshift sphincter she had created in the dragon's chest. The dagger now lay on the floor, just beyond her reach. She hardly had time to be dismayed, though: Something was poking its way out of the hole in the creature's chest, a cluster of pink and grey tubes, some sectioned, others smooth, thicknesses running from thin coil to waggling sausage.

Once free from constriction, the impossibly long, still unwinding organs fanned out, darting in and around each other in graceful slipknots.

When they reached their full length, which was perhaps four feet, violet and yellow bulbs formed at the tips, hatching like boiling popcorn kernels to reveal festering, mucus-covered claw tips of a purplish hue.

Mary Ellen doubted the dagger was even worth retrieving.

The adrenaline surge she had felt at the momentary besting

of the beast fled, and she now fell faint and despairing against the wall, welcoming the mindless safety of hysteria as She came calling, offering the succour of Her embrace.

Before Mary Ellen could entirely surrender to the salve of madness, however, she was rescued by the aching of her scraped palms, transforming into a sweet throb, licked by a cool wet issue that now came spilling extravagantly forth.

Just as had happened after her nightmare session in the dungeon, a shimmer of blood now wept from each palm. This time, though, the red would be a mere peep before the scream to come, once those intestinal pseudopods wrapped her in a final embrace, snuffling, probing, pricking; widening the paths to all her secret places, all the easier to suck her insides out. Looking at the awful creature, she was touched with the knowledge that this was its evil way and its predator nature.

"Take me, then. I don't care," she whispered, not even hearing her own voice. Mary Ellen relaxed, ready to die, sliding down the wall, arms open, bloody palms limp against her thighs.

The tendrils leaped exultantly forward, and the snout behind them seemed to twist in a smug grin.

Mary Ellen felt a sudden yanking inside her palms, a sharp pulling that touched the root of every nerve under her flesh. She watched in terrified, disgusted, delighted amazement as a tidal wave of blood, shivery like jelly, engulfed the attacking viscera.

The animated stigmata roiled about the foul, abominable limbs, obscuring them until they were harmlessly buried shadows. Inside the blood domain, the hungry limbs were compressed down to spidery black fossils that within a few swift moments had crumbled away completely and were lost in the pure sea of red.

Task complete, the blood reliquified itself in mid-air, splashing forward in defiance of the laws of gravity, soaking the now-gaping chest of the stunned dragon.

A moment later the torn scales around the sphincter were dry and grey; the blood had disappeared as if sucked inside the dragon's body.

Mary Ellen barked with hostile delight when the stigmatic blood made a grand reappearance, shooting in crimson jets from every orifice the creature owned, and immediately heating up to a fine red steam that dissolved in the air.

The creature finally fell over on its back, and she stifled a sob. Snuffling as she waited, terrified that like in all good horror movies, the dragon had one more curtain call to make.

When the corpse remained unmoving, Mary Ellen crawled forward, right past it. Dead, the thing was nothing more than disgusting, awkwardly twisted with its belly up and its claws open and limp.

She was reminded of a photo she had seen in the newspaper. A fifty-year-old alligator had been lunching on hunting dogs in the Everglades, until it swallowed a radio collar that led a vengeful posse of hunters right to it. In the picture, they surrounded the gutted monster, rifles held tightly across their chests. Man protecting his dominion.

She made it to Axel's side. His ruddy complexion had given way to a ephemeral blue, and his chest was still. In exhaustion and horror, Mary Ellen began to sob, beating her fist against her breast and then, once the violence of her grief broke, running a trembling hand across the biker's ruined chest.

The bent pin of a Harley badge stuck her, and she welcomed the sharp, minor pain. Carefully, trying hard to ignore the glistening organs and gristle inside the open flesh, she stole the badge from Axel's shredded, blood-soaked denim vest.

The jukebox howl finally subsided, as another selection was dialled up. In the brief moment of quiet, a faint crackling drew her attention to the other side of the toilet, where the dragon corpse's entire musculature was now collapsing, gone

spindly and simple, making a forward retreat through the evolutionary forests. Going human, or some decrepit, badly fashioned approximation of it. By the end, there was only a figure
made out of ash.

A prickling of her skin made Mary Ellen fear her trial had
not ended, however; evidently a new presence was about to
assert itself.

She clutched the badge tightly in her fist. The air in the bathroom, rank with excretion and fluids both human and inhuman, now started spiralling in on itself, streaming crackling past
her cheek, cleansed by a bleeding golden light from nowhere.

The air was nearly sucked out of Mary Ellen's lungs; she
sought refuge under the porcelain sink, which still precariously
hung at a crazy angle from the struggle of only a few moments
ago. The cool water that trickled onto her face from a wrenched-
free pipe convinced her that none of the horror had been a
dream, not even whatever it was that was happening now.

Mary Ellen thought of a childhood weekend spent at the
Jersey shore, when she had woken up one Saturday morning
to black skies filling the window of her parents' rental cottage,
and a wall of clammy air so thick in her tiny bedroom it
seemed as if winter had come to steal away the summer. By
that afternoon, a hurricane had destroyed three cottages less
than a mile away from their vacation home.

Hurricanes do not occur in women's rooms. But then, she rea-
soned, *neither do dragons.*

As the invisible spiral turned more swiftly, the keening wail
of displaced air grew in prominence, building to a chorus of
ghostly whistles that presently ceased as abruptly as if someone had thrown a switch. She couldn't imagine how the noise
hadn't been heard outside in the bar, and why no one had
come to see the matter.

The wind had ceased, as well, and for a long instant there

was nothing but pregnant stillness.

Then, defying whatever reason Mary Ellen still clung to, the cramped loo was filled by a group of at least a dozen women.

They resembled each other closely enough in aspect and dress to be sisters, and had simultaneously materialised out of nowhere, seeming to ride in on the crest of the weird, miniature storm.

In the sudden mob, Mary Ellen couldn't properly count heads, though she had the feeling there were many more of them than she could see, than could possibly fit.

Despite their feminine forms, however, the tall, sleek creatures were not quite human. What Mary Ellen had thought at first glance to be golden girdles adorning their tiny waists and large busts were actually some sort of swooping, vaguely insectoid carapace, an elegant exoskeleton that gleamed with a sweet-looking fluid.

As well, the long single braid hanging down each broad back was not woven from any sort of human hair. The strands were ten times too thick, resembling bundles of copper wire. A faint electricity danced in and out of each immaculate series of Celtic knots, fireflies against the rich hues of dried blood.

The women's faces boasted a nominally human bone structure, but all the details had been simplified; no lines or creases or imperfections, features wiped clean of fault and any accompanying proof of personality.

As Mary Ellen gaped, a blinding radiance began to pour from their eye-sockets in waves that expanded on contact with the air, the light seeking itself out like a living thing and melting together until the tiny room became painfully bright, its air thick with a damp miasma that twinkled green and blue. The temperature had dropped so far that her teeth chattered.

Look at them, like they're fresh from the beehive. How many, how many? Mary Ellen wondered. More than she could count, all impossibly crowded together, yet not jostling each other, serene and beautiful, standing in a practised formation, forming a seashell spiral with Axel's body at the core.

In one inhumanly brilliant moment of choreography, they all simultaneously grasped hands. Mary Ellen noticed that their long, slim fingers were smooth and sharp at the tips, with no nails.

Axel's body was nearly obscured by these alien women; from her vantage point she saw only one leg from the knee down, blue jeans drenched with life's blood, black boot scuffed and dotted with many shiny, coin-sized droplets.

Dozens of golden throats began to vibrate, a sweet wordless chant building until it filled the air, unbroken by the need for breath. Mary Ellen raptly drew her knees up beneath her chin, her grief forgotten, overtaken by a warm sense of wonder and, oddly enough, triumph. She now realised these things meant neither her nor Axel any harm. In fact, they didn't even seem to be aware of her presence. Or else chose not to acknowledge it.

When the chanting reached a peak it multiplied into a chord the likes of which she had never heard; a burst of celestial static, perhaps, or a plane the size of a world leaving its runway.

A barely perceptible spasm jostled Axel's visible leg, and then the entire centre of the spiral of women where his body lay nestled became engulfed in a golden-white fire.

Mary Ellen could feel the heat against her arms and legs, like in those sunny August days spent out on the beach when she was still small, and happy.

The flames resolved into a crackling ball of joyous energy, which began travelling outwards through the women's bodies, possessing each unmoving form for only a moment before rolling into the next, leaving each fresh host steaming and smoking from the intensity, smoke curling from their fingers and braids.

The ball of flame reached the last woman, who stood not five feet away from where Mary Ellen cowered. She flinched back against the slippery tile wall, afraid the flame would next tumble towards her. She squeezed her eyes shut in fear.

When she opened them, the golden women were gone, and the fire, too. All that was left was Axel's broken body on the other side of the women's room, still gory, but now somehow less tragic. Just old meat, waiting to be disposed of.

Mary Ellen's still warm cheeks tingled as a fresh curtain of cool tears fell across them. Her grief at Axel's death seemed softened, somehow more bearable.

Though she had troubling believing the event that she had just witnessed, the situation rang familiar enough from her childhood readings of Viking mythology. Could these golden creatures in fact be Valkyries, the goddesses which came to conduct the souls of brave warriors fallen in battle to the halls of Valhalla, where their reward awaited?

Mary Ellen allowed herself a single laugh of disbelief, wondering how much weirder it all could possibly get.

Then she realised that the aura of the benign creatures had faded away, and she was still left in the men's room of a biker bar with two corpses — well, one corpse and a pile of ash. Her sense of urgency returned. Seized with the instinct towards flight, she first wanted Axel's knife back.

Stepping gingerly, careful not to slip in the gore, she made her way past the biker's now empty corpse and over to the charred mess that he had died trying to save her from, the half-reptile, half-human thing that she knew would have cracked her bones and sucked them dry if allowed its natural way.

She tried to hate the thing for what it had done to Axel, but her hostility, though deep, was disappointingly impersonal. Staring at the stupid remains, she found she could despise this monster no more greatly than a rabid animal, a scorpion or a rattlesnake.

Heart in her mouth, she reached down and clasped the wire pommel of the long iron dagger with both hands. Inside the ash, there was evidently still a core that had not been entirely blasted. The blade dragged free with a wet, raw sound, and a grey and pink organ was dragged part way free, shivering gelatinously in a momentary parody of animation that made her gasp.

The blade wiped reasonably clean against the rough, drooping hand towel that dangled from its metal box next to the sink. Secreting the dagger inside her long leather coat, she checked her face in the mirror to remind herself of her own identity, and left the women's room.

She had expected the worse: several tables worth of stoned and beery bikers and their bitches staring up at her in quizzical disbelief, wanting to know what the fuck had just gone on in the can.

But, Mary Ellen realised with a start, despite the apocalypse she had survived, it was still not even midnight, on a weeknight. The place was between drinking shifts; the day labourers who sucked down whiskey and drafts into the early evening had tottered home to their old ladies, and the dealers and unemployed were somewhere in their cribs, just now going through the most casual grooming in preparation for another night of abusing their livers.

The back room of Seven-Seventeen stood mercifully empty; the over-amped jukebox was playing a Metallica CD for the benefit of metalhead alcoholics not yet arrived. She felt like going over and kicking it right in the speaker.

Mary Ellen drew herself together and affected the most casual stroll she could to the front bar. There was no one left there she knew. Evidently Axel hadn't thought he would need any back up. But then, she knew that he hadn't seen the dragon the way she had. Nobody could.

The bartenders had changed shifts, and Mary Ellen had to ask a girl to move so she could get her long overcoat off the stool where Axel had left it. She then strolled out of Seven Seventeen, leaving a good friend and a little piece of hell behind her.

VII

As Mary Ellen Masters immediately learned, however, respite was not at hand.

Eighth Street was an implacable stream of pale neon, leaking gaseous from store windows across her path. She hustled past mouldering walk-ups where the lichen taunted her with its black light glow, competing with the diseased hues of drug addiction, incipient schizophrenia, despair and megalomania, an onrushing gulf yawning to receive her as she careened off the shoulders of disgusted punks and shocked college students, not even feeling the occasional remonstrative clip to her shoulder or the back of her head by an irritated dealer of faux bud or a coked-up and tweaking transvestite on her way to Stingy Lou-Lou's, the freak sanctuary by the park that so self-consciously masqueraded as a fifties-style diner.

Though all the bitter sickness rolled into her belly like a gauntleted fist, her nausea was kept at bay by the sheer animal fear conjured by the much more profound threat of The

Black, threads of it sinuously interwoven into the unpleasant river of humanity she was slogging upstream against, as if it were a feather of tainted blood drawn up into a hypodermic of stepped-on dope, cheaply evil with its dismal, milky taint.

Before she could reverse her momentum, she fell against a haggard bum that had darted from the garbage-can shadows by an ancient tenement to block her path. The vapour of darkness leaked from his pores even more potently than the stink of his filthy clothes and a month's worth of sweat; she stared at the torn, colourless parka drawn across his chest and saw the ghosts of bristly fur that slept beneath his flesh, patiently waiting the few more evenings to go until freedom, freedom to know the pleasures of The Feeding.

That was what it was called; she heard it in his mind. *The Feeding.* That was what the dragon had been about to do to her. And now here was another monster, thankfully not yet hungry.

Even the low, unnatural growl that made his Adam's Apple bubble like melting plastic wasn't enough to draw her eyes up to meet his gaze; to look straight into the eyes of The Black yet again would be enough to overwhelm her, send her fainting to the hard pavement, against the hard, mouldy pile of pitbull turds she was vaguely aware lurked at her feet, a few feet short of the fenced-in plot of greenery where it might have eventually sunk into the mulch.

The discordant strains of the werewolf's surprised challenge resonated against each other in three distinguishable octaves, and Mary Ellen was crazily reminded of the Disney version of *Pinocchio*, of that wicked mall filled with little boys turned into puppy dogs and put up for sale. She saw specks of dirt moving through the peppery thatch of hair crisscrossing the not yet hungry Feeder's partially exposed chest. They moved, and she realised they were fleas.

Lurching, nearly losing her balance on a slick patch of ice, Mary Ellen got past him, nearly toppling an old Polish woman with her shopping cart in the process.

Daring a look back once she was a few yards away, the hairs on the back of her neck prickled at the sight of the Feeder, who was standing there still, but now with his head thrown back, the tips of his long ears quivering where they poked out from his matted mess of long hair sprouting from under a colourless, oversized watch cap. Preparing for a hunt, or in communication with the pack? Were these things everywhere?

She thought of The Black, that great force of evil she had felt, and now saw it as a tribal enemy armed with the fetid blessings of a fallen angel, the taste of darkness and flesh and souls on their flicking inhuman tongues, feeding a thousand different ways on human sheep.

The Black was a great wave rolling in from somewhere out in the void, and now here it was breaking around her, threatening to swallow her up and bury her jellied bones in a bed of briny acid. Her death seemed all around her.

Another pang staggered her as she continued across the broad open space of First Avenue, an extravagant number of lanes that demanded pedestrians fall into a lope across or become road kill under the wheels of the unruly, snarling pack of yellow taxis barely held at bay by the light.

Next to one of those taxis was a nondescript pick-up truck with grimed-over New Jersey plates, piloted by a dim shape behind a windscreen mottled brown by the mud of some swampy home a hundred miles away, in the still wilds of the South Jersey Pine Barrens.

The driver gunned the motor, its throaty growl through a blown muffler another announcement of implacable appetite. Mary Ellen stared horrified at the truck even as the light changed, with her still a good fifteen feet from the curb.

Clutch released, the vehicle jerked forward, jockeying with a cab piloted by a fiercely grimacing, turbaned driver. Mary Ellen made it to the curb, the fender passing within a few inches of her shoulders even as she gained the sidewalk.

Looking back, she caught a glimpse of the driver, received a series of impressions: hollowed-out skulls full of knotted viscera, stalkings done for the fun of it through mucky, fly-infested swampland, full meat lockers stained with the red whorls of fingerprints, repeated a hundred times over. A hunter unapprehended thanks to its ageless nature, its feral wisdom beneath the lumpy facade of a watery-eyed, buck-toothed hick with a haircut twenty years out of date. She recognised it for what it was, and it in turn recognised her. And hated her.

She took refuge in an ugly Chinese food joint, of the sort where the most popular platters were displayed in a strikingly unappetising manner on a series of back-lit photographic blow-ups. There was a pay phone on the wall, at least. She would revive herself with a cup of tea and try to figure out who she could call, if *anybody*. Her gaze grew momentarily bleary with tears, thinking how she'd inadvertently led Axel to his fate. Who could possibly be of any help now?

The moon-faced Eurasian teenager behind the pitted counter was sallow and vague, bitter over wasting an evening of her youth confined to her parents' business, blandly taking orders from disdainful, distracted hipsters and wheedling street people. Mary Ellen ordered tea from her.

"*Just* tea?" asked the girl, ringing it up as she spoke, still forced to fill out a receipt even for the cup of hot water and the bag. Mary Ellen nodded distractedly, not interested in the girl's irritated contempt.

Standing at the counter waiting for something hot to shock her senses back into normal mode, she felt her shoulders shake and a gagging at the base of her throat as she realised there were still Black emanations bombarding her from somewhere close by.

She looked around, seeing nothing but a leather-jacketed Ramones clone waiting for takeout, staring idly out the window at the passing parade of potential groupies.

Then the choppy edges of what sounded like a diatribe in Chinese reached her ears, and she became aware of the two men standing in the back of the kitchen, half-obscured from her sight by a pillar.

The thing being disciplined by the angry little man looked human, but Mary Ellen's senses told her it wasn't. In its white cap and apron, hunched over, it attracted no attention tucked away in its station by a quietly sizzling wok, but when she scrutinised it she realised it was a reanimated thing, a doll of flesh no longer alive, at least as she had before this understood the definition of life, powered instead by an ebon electricity and a blind need. Impressionable, equipped with only a primitive logic system, prey to the intentions of even strong-willed humans, as long as they understood its proper care and training.

Mary Ellen was even more dismayed by the accompanying realisation: There had to be some other humans who had inklings of the Black, enough knowledge even to exploit such minor inhabitants. Could it be that the worlds intersected more than she could imagine?

The tearing away of veil after veil since Christmas Eve was threatening to rip out the moorings of her sanity as well, and as she headed for the door, her temporary sanctuary tainted by yet more corruption and hunger, she found herself wishing again for the restfulness of hysteria, freed from the responsibility of caring about the deposition of her body and mind.

On the street, away from the sickly radiance of the Chinese restaurant's fluorescent lights, the moonlight kissed all faces blue, and the cold air stung her cheeks. She felt the Black welling up from every shadow, groping for her, inviting and cajoling her to give herself up and be absorbed, be consumed and perhaps even reborn into a plane of static decay, aimless atrocity and eternal need never quite fulfilled.

She threw down the paper cup of tea in frustration, sighing fretfully when the contents splashed up and left a series of glistening beads across her long black boots. She moaned and clenched her fists, afraid of the street, afraid of the cabs, but terrified to still be here out in the open, embraced by the dark. A beacon of mortality, announcing herself to all the prowling Feeders.

Confused, gripped by a panic demanding immediate flight, she tried to think of a destination. The subway, that was it! Another block and a half, and she'd be to Cooper Square, and the R line. She visualised the subway entrance, yawning open to receive her, to offer a subterranean refuge.

Steeling herself, she strode west, trying not to shudder as she sought to concentrate on the insufficient comfort of the softly glowing streetlights, the faintly mocking warmth of the occasional storefront.

It was better when she reached St. Marks; even though passing by the front of a rock 'n' roll bar, a tourist trap serving four dollar beers, she was struck by a jagged feint from something terribly wrong inside. But the noise and brighter illumination was bracing, and before she knew it, she had made it across to the desolate island in the middle of the square and to the ancient iron mouth that greeted and directed her down to the subway line, a world where the twilight never came, not on the platform or inside of the speeding trains.

She paid her fare and passed through the chrome turnstiles, by now too numb to even feel the steel bar meet her waist and yield to her forward motion. She ignored the leering face of the booth clerk, a fuzzy-cheeked black man who licked his lips at the curve of her full breasts flashing beneath her open coat.

Her brain was preoccupied by a field of buzzing static, as her subconscious laboured to process all she had just felt and witnessed, and free the bottleneck that pulsed in between her perceptions and her reason. When the uptown train pulled up and the doors heaved open, she automatically stepped inside, where it was all lit up, and she was safe from the niggling threat of the open space of the tunnel at either ends of the platform, where The Black snickered and pulsed. Though the train would travel right through it, at least she was protected by several feet of solid steel, and the constant vigilance of the lights.

She collapsed onto a hard plastic bench, her supporting hand just missing a shallow pool of some unidentifiable clear fluid. Shuddering, she lurched across the aisle to a cleaner seat.

The doors sighed closed, the rubber bumpers thudding reassuringly. The train started up with a slight, gentle lurch; an assured pilot was in the tiny booth, not pressured at this hour to try and stay close to schedule.

The whining of the wheels built as the train rocketed off into the tunnel, and as the view out the windows went to black, Mary Ellen worried if she had done the wrong thing.

The more she sat there on the train, the more frightened she was to leave it, and go back up into the voracious night. In the end, she stayed there until dawn, not allowing herself to sleep, eyes averting from the shrieking dark and unaccountable rattles from outside and beneath the restlessly roaming subway car.

VIII

Reeling with fatigue from spending the night switching subway lines so she wouldn't be kicked off the trains, too afraid of human predators to even catnap, Mary Ellen was feeling dull and stupid when she met her first angel, there on the corner of Second Avenue and Houston.

Hiking up the spit and piss-stained concrete steps of the subway stop, she was eager to ascend from inside the earth once the dawn had safely arrived. Her own sharp gasps rang in her ears, and she could see her exhalations crystallise in the cold dawn air.

Pivoting at the head of the stairs to avoid a homeless entrepreneur's filthy blanket scattered with an unappealing assortment of trash-picked goods, Mary Ellen turned abruptly to head towards her home and instead yelped with surprise.

For a moment, she felt like she was out of her body, floating above Houston Street and looking down: Hovering somewhere above the awesome apparition, able to observe its every detail, judge its scale against the broad, four-lane street.

The glow around the creature was vivid and stunning even in daylight. Blue fire fringed by pinkish-grey sparks blazed around a hugely proportioned figure seemingly constructed out of iron slag. Chrome patterns of what was either sigils or circuitry were laid over the top of it in complex patterns that the longer gazed at, compelled Mary Ellen further and further into a charged state of excited pleasure. From the moment she saw it, she knew this thing was not of The Black.

The longer she looked the further she fell into a vertiginous rapture. The centre of the apparition's chest was peeled back, revealing a subcutaneous layer of ropy, woven veins that vibrated every time the angel would take a breath.

Wings, or the black shadows of them, were tucked behind gleaming barbed-wire shoulder blades. Imposing yet insubstantial things — unsettling, hazy scoops of darkness that seemed as if they must be folded in on themselves many times, and if spread to their full span might stretch from one side of Houston to the other. Or perhaps even never end.

Its serene and distant blue features formed an impassive mask leaking painful brilliance from the eyes, the mouth, thin nostrils. No hair grew anywhere on its head or body. An extravagant number of fingers and toes ended in long, graceful digits that looked sleekly metallic.

And the crotch was smooth and sexless. Mary Ellen found herself, in the very midst of her gape-jawed shock oddly disappointed, then dizzy from the clash of such a prosaic thought with the surreal sense of wonder this vision inspired.

But then, who wouldn't want the chance to see what an angel's cock looked like?

As she watched, the angel drew itself up to full height, at least fifteen feet. A great gust of amber-smelling wind heralded the spreading of those majestic wings, which now open indeed seemed to swoop forever in a profound arc soaring far above the heads of the unwary pedestrians crossing the little traffic island.

Their symmetry seduced her somewhere deep in her belly, filled her throat with an oddly peaceful excitement. For the first time in her life, she felt the presence of other worlds. Something she had never expected, never felt even kneeling before the rail as her tongue cushioned the insufferable dryness of the Host slid in by oversize, warm fingers.

She wanted to speak, but every atom of her corporeality was held in stasis by a numbing field of electricity. Her eyeballs began to dry from her inability to blink.

All the nightmarish insanities she had suffered until this moment were superseded, reduced to thin memories of merely unpleasant tribulations. The magical new awareness she had endlessly cursed now seemed, rather than a disease or disability, a supremely wonderful gift: Like the gold ring, hidden beneath her tights, piercing the nubbin of her clit had first seemed, when an old boyfriend had tugged it shortly after it healed.

Vibrating in sympathy to the field generated by the awesome creature, that soft metal felt as though it were spinning in place, churning up a fiery friction in her most tender flesh.

The images of great burning wheels bifurcating the skies of a much younger planet burst in sharp relief upon her brain; she saw mud-caked, toothless shepherds dwarfed by a fleet of such machines, cowering in awe and terror.

And now she saw a snake immense beyond conception evidently motionless in the vast celestial emptiness, jaws that yawned deeper than any earthbound canyon closing around its own huge, blunt tail. The endless revelation pounding outside of time's flow that now engulfed her resembled an orgasm, but only in the way that a puny desert lizard's ephemeral biology echoed an extinct dinosaur's grandeur.

Like a blessing, she could see the angel for what it was, knowing it to be created out of the same fire that burned in that massive serpent's great unseeing eye, the same flames that had danced and looped across the sky-consuming wheels, that now pulsed within her insignificant body like an invading isotope of purest radiation.

Trembling with the effort of the slightest movement, Mary Ellen raised a hand towards the great creature before her, which was still poised in the middle of the street, wings at full attention as if preparing for flight.

At her effort the angel actually looked down at her, evidencing through an odd turn of its head an expression that in a human being might qualify as mild surprise. Mary Ellen registered a quick impression of a truly alien process, far more strange and incomprehensible than the corrupt reptilian wiles of the dragon in the bar, or the insect-like serenity of the Valkyries in the women's room.

When their gazes met Mary Ellen felt her body explode. Every dazzled atom seemed to be repelled from the one next to it. She found herself experiencing a complete awareness of every organ in her body, its weight, its shape, its place in the secret web each person carried and to which was, mercifully, mostly numb. She felt herself slip free from the entire wet, sucking, pumping clockwork thing as if she had merely peeled off a dirty stocking.

Then she was truly within the angel's embrace, and could name it: her mind translated the information into a word that looked like "Haniel," or perhaps "Onoel." What it really meant was: "He who can see God."

And now she could see he who sees God. She could also see the world that stood behind him, that rotated beneath their theoretical embrace. The creature was one of seven or perhaps ten like it that shared a common identity...archangels? She had heard the term before, but not really understood it until now.

She understood that this was a proud creature who was humiliated by its very contact with the base plain that had been all Mary Ellen had, until this moment, ever known.

By its nature, however, such visits were its charge. It was attracted to Mary Ellen in particular by ringing sympathies that in the clearness of her floating consciousness she saw had been vibrating since the moment of her birth, during an unseasonably cool Labour Day weekend twenty-seven years ago.

A portion of Haniel's shimmering blue mind lazily tugged at Mary Ellen now, offering to take her deeper into its embrace. She knew without doubt she would be safe from all harm there, and that further and greater enigmas would begin to unfold in an unbroken chain.

She feared the result. As harrowing as her life had suddenly become, the new idea of releasing herself from the only reality she had ever known, and possibly never returning, was enough to inspire a small bubble of fear.

And once that bubble popped, it spilled forth a clear astringent that doused the blinding flames in Mary Ellen's heart, and she found herself back on Second Avenue and Houston Street, being bumped about by a stream of young commuters seeking the subway entrance's open mouth. A man with a neatly trimmed goatee and horn-rimmed glasses carrying an artist's portfolio glanced back over his shoulder as he hurried down the steps, obviously wondering what drug she was on.

She stumbled out of the relentless path of the professional bohemians and sought the safety of a nearby public bench, ignoring the hugely fat bum that took up fully half of the rough wooden seat.

Mary Ellen sat there, arms folded across her belly, retching and gagging, her long leather coat drawn tightly around her. She wanted to vomit but was dismally aware that she had not eaten in hours, and there would be nothing to force up but a painful, burning trickle of bile. She was embarrassed to be sharing this moment of her post-angelic inebriation and withdrawal with her fellow New Yorker.

Not that he was helping; his odour was magnificent. Body sweat trapped inside an extravagant collection of mouldering wool and colourless cloth, leavened by an unexpected dash of some sickly-sweet incense. She could feel him looking at her, but she refused to make eye contact.

"Sister, you been seein' some heavenly hosts, I bet."

The strikingly mellifluous bass flowed from beside her in warm, amused tones, betraying only a hint of hard living's strain.

Startled, she looked him in the face. His skin was moderately dark, but heavily mottled with a riot of ashy explosions betraying the difficulties that faced him in securing regular scrubbing opportunities. His nappy hair was overgrown nearly to the point of shapelessness, and made profound by a profusion of grey highlights.

The gaze out of one yellowed, veiny eye reflected an almost fatherly concern. The other eye was blind, covered in a thick cataract that insisted on shadow despite the direct glare of the early morning sun.

"I been there, honey, it ain't no matter. There is indeed more things on heaven an' earth, all right? Some of us just allowed to see more of it than others."

Mary Ellen didn't know what to say. Her Sight was indeed still with her; she knew the man was nothing more or less than what he seemed; not one of some hungry or hostile predator race in disguise. But that didn't help her figure whether he was just another rambling substance abuser or — wouldn't it be a shred of hope if this were so — another seer.

A thought suddenly occurred to her: How many of the rambling, shambling wrecks infesting the city's streets, babbling about secret worlds and conspiracies, were only insane? Already, she had fought the temptation to just let go, plummet into the pit of incoherence and confusion where none of this would matter.

With bittersweet humour, she pictured herself coming to sit on this very bench for the remainder of her life, leaving only to excrete or plunder garbage cans for food.

"You don't know what to say to big old Benjamin, do ya little daughter? That's okay, I'm way over takin' any offence. Just tryin' to offer a little friendly advice."

His huge head turned away, and lolled back the few inches the fat neck that supported it would allow.

"I come out here every day and turn my face up to God, hope He melt away this damn caul keep me seein' straight. I know that if I be patient, He get around to me. He get around to all of us. Him or Mr. Scratch, that's for sure."

Mary Ellen tried to clear her throat, but it was still dry from the spell that had just finished riding her, and her voice came out as an embarrassing squeak.

"Do you ... see things?" She coughed dryly.

Benjamin laughed, digging in his pocket as if in answer. Instead he produced a still-sealed package of honey-flavoured cough drops, which he proffered with a flourish.

"Here, honey, start me out on this box. January be one nasty month to be on the streets, and somebody who talks as much as me always got to keep his throat workin'."

Gratefully, Mary Ellen accepted the gift, though it took her numb fingers a few moments of fumbling to strip away the cellophane. Benjamin gently chided her.

"Yeah, it get cold out here, you don't keep movin' around. That's what happen, you stand right over there in the middle of the street, not movin' an inch while that nasty-ass winter wind go whippin' up and down the street. Way that sucker wailed, I suspect we ready for another big snow storm 'fore evenin'."

"How long was I standing there?"

Benjamin grinned widely.

"Honey child, I didn't *think* you knew! You looked just like my great grand ma-ma, when one of her spells take her, they supposed to only come during the services but you can't be tellin' God when you're ready to talk to him, he don't need no appointment, that's right.

"Great grannie be peelin' potatoes over the bucket one evenin', and near cut her finger right off, she goes into a state. And I was pissin' in my little pants, cuz I'm the only one there, runnin' the potatoes in from the porch, where it was nice and cool, to the hot kitchen where gran and mama be cookin' up Sunday's best.

"But she don't even flinch, just sits there in place starin' ahead, this satisfied little smile crinklin' that old mouth, and breathin' these little noises which I just couldn't quite make out as words, and meanwhile there's all this blood jumpin' all over this place, sprayin' right into the bucket of potatoes.

"I ran and got my mama, and she and Gran came rushin' back, upset but not surprised like. Instead they just put a blanket around her while they tie up that finger, not even speakin' to her, like they know she wouldn't hear.

"Half an hour later great Gran snaps right up and says, 'Ouch!' and looks down at her bandaged hand, and near about faints."

Benjamin nodded toward the subway entrance.

"I seen that same look on your face, little girl, though you a damn sight prettier than great Gran was at that time, rest her sweet soul."

Mary Ellen shivered and got up from the bench, faced Benjamin and returned his cough drops.

"Thanks a lot, Benjamin. You're a very nice man."

He captured her small, blue-white hand between his grimy, oversized grey paws. She didn't mind; there was nothing threatening in the gesture.

"You tell that to my two ex-wives, you see 'em. I could use a character witness."

They laughed together, and she waved once from the far corner of Second Avenue.

When she got back to her apartment, she locked all three locks on the door and even wedged the night bar in place. The last two days' mail were consigned to the kitchen table sight unseen; if the earth was indeed flat, squeezed between the fists of heaven and hell, how much attention did the phone company really warrant?

Feeling every coat of sweat and tears burying the pores of her face, she wanted to shower clean, but her step turned numb and drunken before she could even make it to the bathroom.

Thirty-six hours later, she awoke on top of her unmade bed, her boots still on her feet and clumsily tangled in a taffy of blankets. She couldn't remember getting there from the bathroom, or any dreams that might have come. Her pillow, however was soaked and discoloured by a pungent bile.

IX

New York City Police Detective lieutenant Mickey O'Farrell stood in stunned disbelief before the unholy mess in Seven Seventeen's women's room. Snorting, he rubbed the back of his hand against his nose, and tried not to sneeze.

His eyes watered a little, startling him. He, of all his associates, should have been the least likely to have been staggered by the extravagant display of blood and viscous fluids that had already started to emanate the perfume of rot.

Maybe he was developing some sort of allergy; it seemed everyone else on the force had one; to various plants, to dairy products, to small domestic animals. A true sign of decadence for him, if so; one of the many dolorous prices of civilisation.

Arnie Marasheek, the precinct's Iranian forensics man, looked up sheepishly from where he was painstakingly scraping bits of congealed gore into an evidence vial. Strings of black hair were pasted down by sweat against his nut-brown skull, and his blues were black with half-moons under the arms.

"What a fucking big mess, Mr. Mickey. It's as if I have been looking for proof of a rape in a whorehouse. I haven't even figured out the murder weapon," Marasheek complained. O'Farrell's fellow immigrant affected a proper Oxford English, taught him by his parents. It was dying the slow death against the all-compassing New Yawk patois of his fellow officers, though.

Mostly, he was an incredibly efficient policeman, and often the first on the scene of a murder; known for his straightforward zeal even in other precincts.

Which sometimes proved a problem for O'Farrell. Though he liked the little monkey well enough, he was never happy to draw him on an investigation.

"We have what appears by his vest to be the member of a motorcycle club, suffering multiple gashes and contusions, as well as what appears to be a broken neck. Of course I'm just an evidence man, but that's my opinion. We also have this dumpy old fellow, he looks as if he could have wandered over from the Bowery."

"Who's here from the coroner?" O'Farrell demanded, shrugging his shoulder hard enough to soothingly crack his massive spine.

Marasheek grimaced at the noise.

"Whom do you think? The very proper Mr. So and So, isn't this fascinating, just, pip-pip cheerio."

Pennington, the Englishman. Arnie hated all Britishers, thanks to having been raised in London, where he'd been thrashed regularly by bully boys and skinheads.

The funny thing was, Arnie and Howard Pennington shared something in common; both had the odd knack for being on call at just the right time to pull the truly messy ones, the stuff that even the Post reporters can't do justice. Mexican newspaper stuff. Pennington also relished his job, always dropping deadpan one-liners with droll precision. O'Farrell liked his sense of humour. For an Englishman.

The gig was obviously going to take Arnie forever. The women's room was so small that no more than two men could work in there at a time, for fear of disturbing the unpleasant evidence that had been so lavishly splattered all across the filthy, scuffed tile and discoloured porcelain.

"Hold your nose and keep shovelling, Arnie," he advised the evidence man, who shook his head in disgust, not bothering to look back up. Before O'Farrell turned away he noted a confusion of foot prints near the door. Gazing at the various tread marks and scuffs, he speculated that the missing party in this bloody incident was small-statured, from the size of the unaccounted-for footprints. Female?

He was going to have to do some real work, it seemed, with his two pesky, alert fellow officers around. O'Farrell's dismay was deep. He was *hungry*.

His most recent meal had been nearly twenty hours ago. A bag lunch carried from home, engulfed while he was squeezed into an unmarked, pulling stakeout duty at a Lower East Side squat infested with anarchists who had threatened to burn the crumbling building down before they'd let the city drive them out.

He was on the case because one of the squatters was a known associate of Daniel Rakowitz, the infamous Butcher of Tompkins Square Park. The schizophrenic, chicken-handling street trash had killed his snotty ballet student roommate and cooked her up into a stew which he fed to the homeless that in those lax years had been allowed to camp out in the one of the East Village's only shreds of greenery.

Meeting him in his holding cell hours after he was arrested, O'Farrell had stared Rakowitz right in the eye when the wild-eyed, speed-damaged hippie claimed he hadn't committed the murder at all, and that it was the work of his friendly neighbourhood Satanic cult.

"That's bullshit, Danny. The only Satanic cult in the East Village is a stupid bunch of dirty hippie junkies that can barely get up to pee, much less kill somebody. But you know what? You didn't do it. I know that."

Rakowitz had opened his mouth in shock, ready to babble. But O'Farrell rumbled onward, that day, with the tape recorder punched off, against regulation.

"But you're going to pay for it anyway. Someone has to. Don't worry, Dannyboy. We'll try and get you declared insane."

Rakowitz and his scuzzy pals were harmless. O'Farrell knew it better than anyone possibly could, but thanks to the persistent rumours, fuelled by the idiots in the press, six years later he was still dutifully checking out leads. That's what happened when the papers got their dirty hands on a simple situation.

Rakowitz, unwilling to play along but too terrified of Mickey to change his story, was proclaiming his innocence to this day; and the tabs faithfully provided yearly coverage of his petition for parole.

And so indirectly through his own action it had been eighteen hours before this, his massive frame stuck in the tiny, stripped-down sedan, O'Farrell had been gnawing disconsolately on a chilled shinbone from a homeboy rapist that he'd found trying to hide by burying himself in the sand under a Coney Island boardwalk the week before.

Grousing to himself then that no matter how tender she had been, that goddamn dancer had ended up more trouble than she was worth.

"Well, well, hello there, Mickey. It certainly does appear as if we've been granted another New York Post headline to add to our resumes," Dr. Howard Pennington announced himself, in light, clipped tones, gesturing with his polished chrome clipboard toward the mess O'Farrell had turned his back to, thinking to gratefully depart.

Over the shorter man's shoulder, the detective saw that the uniforms were still detaining the bartender, the bar back, and six disgruntled customers for the next round of questioning.

"Pennington. You must be friends with the meat wagon jockey," O'Farrell said. Pennington chuckled perfunctorily and pushed into the room, ushering the much larger detective back in.

"Let's take a good look at what we've got," Pennington suggested. O'Farrell sighed. He had hoped to at least lean over the bar and draw himself a weak, human-brewed draught, and least smooth the edge of his hunger. Limey fuck.

Instead, drawing his trousers loose so he wouldn't tear yet another pair, O'Farrell knelt beside the closest body; the grisly remains of what had been a sturdy biker, his long hair and beard now matted dark with gore. By the sharp angle his head rested against his shoulder, O'Farrell immediately knew it had been snapped. Looking closer, he found five bruises on the neck.

He immediately deduced the biker had not been killed by a human being. And having come to that conclusion, the next thing he noticed was the smell.

Perhaps he had been distracted by his hunger, or by the native stink of the piss-stained floorboards. But now he realised he had subconsciously detected the odour the moment he came into the bathroom: the sickly sweet spoor of a Feeder.

His nostrils flared as he gulped a deep breath, and was nearly staggered by the strength of it. Like his own body odour, yet more ephemeral in its power. Redolent of a certain otherworldliness.

"Looks like some of the *bros* got into a disagreement,"

Pennington said, running a rubber-gloved hand over the dead man's throat in a vaguely sensual way that made Arnie Marasheek, over next to the other body, turn his head in repulsion.

"I'd like to see the size of the one that did this," O'Farrell said.

"A bruiser," Pennington agreed. O'Farrell shut his eyes a moment, rocking on the balls of his feet. Small footprints, though. Well, that was no matter. A Feeder didn't have to be big to be deadly. The Feeder spoor was strewn all over this corpse, and from the abundance of it filling the room, the other body, too. In fact, O'Farrell had never smelled it quite this badly, not even around one of them.

Struck by a horrible suspicion, the ogre duckwalked the three steps to the other side of the bathroom, where the other meat lay. When his hands made contact with the tacky blood crusting the shredded sweatshirt the corpse was wearing, the bristly coils of hair on the back of his hand prickled, and he felt his mouth fill with water.

As soon as he saw the wound, he knew. Puckered, extravagantly black flesh was sloughed back as if it had been melted by some intense fire, cauterised so there was no blood. It was a stab wound; the mark of iron. He was looking at something rare: A Feeder corpse.

He gingerly put two fingers out, and pressed against the body's chest, right above the wound. The corpse's face mournfully rebuked him with its dour sagging jowls, even as the hole in its chest swelled, flesh puckering until the clear, glistening head of a death grub poked tentatively out into the air, its arrival accompanied by a soft hiss.

O'Farrell could hear Pennington gasp and stumble back, causing Arnie to look up from his station at the old man's feet.

"Oh shit," he cried, pausing for a shiver before scrambling for the door himself. "What the fuck is *that*?"

O'Farrell answered gently, condescendingly. His hunger had momentarily been chased away by wonderment and apprehension.

"*The worms crawl in, the worms crawl out.*"

"There can't be larval activity this soon, and besides, I've never seen anything like that bollocky bastard before," Pennington complained in a weak, nauseated voice from his shelter on the other side of the doorjamb.

"Maybe there's some kind of cracked septic tank beneath this shithole. Who knows. Shut your eyes if you're scared, little boys. I'll get rid of the thing."

Pennington began to protest: "Maybe we should keep it for — "

"Shut up and go get that bartender to get me a double whiskey," O'Farrell ordered. Pennington held his ground defiantly; the moment's tension was broken when Arnie sighed, shook his head, and hightailed it to the bar.

It was a healthy sucker, O'Farrell conceded. At least an inch thick, each plate of its carapace shivering with the gelid sinew that pulsed beneath it. The entire disgusting affair capped off with that flattened out, clear wet skull, the wire-thin feeding tubes sprouting around the base like whiskers.

He found Feeder biology repulsive. He didn't mind parasites too much — he enjoyed flattening the fleas and ticks he farmed from his hairy body between the stony pads of two fingers. But the more esoteric the race in question, it seemed the more gothic and unpleasant their surrounding ecology.

To host a death grub of this heft, the de-animated Feeder sprawled in his own deathblood on the bathroom floor must have been truly ancient, his bloodline conceivably reaching back to the time of the big reptiles.

"Here you go, Mr. Mickey," Arnie said from over his shoulder, slipping the glass into O'Farrell's open hand.

"Thanks. Now light me a pack of matches, a whole pack," Mickey instructed, still watching the death grub pondering a course of action. In a moment it would decide to retreat; if it had finished eating it would be time to lay eggs.

Arnie refused to look straight on at the thing, cowering a healthy distance back as he lit a souvenir pack of matches from one of the upscale strip clubs.

"Damn, there goes a guaranteed blowjob, up in smoke," he complained.

"You should keep a little black book. Be more organised."

O'Farrell dashed the alcohol all over the grub; before Pennington could raise another protest Arnie had tossed the lit matches at it. The grub went up in emerald flames immediately; as O'Farrell knew, its kind secreted an acidic oil that burnt harder than petroleum.

The initial burst of green fire singed O'Farrell's eyebrows, but he didn't flinch, and the jade tongues receded quickly, leaving the dead Feeder's torso reduced to an even more brittle, blackened state. Mickey knew that by tomorrow the corpse would be nothing but dust, if there was no reanimation ritual.

Fuck that, he thought. He didn't even know the thing.

The little footprints. Two Feeders in a row over a meal? Doubtful. There was no shortage of livestock to go around. And then the wound: A Feeder would never carry iron. That was tempting the lightning, the terrible swift sword. Could it have been a human being?

As unlikely as it seemed, there was that possibility. His appetite restated its case deep in his belly as he thought it would certainly be interesting to meet a human who knew the secret of iron.

O'Farrell enjoyed the tiny warmth of the Filipino whore beneath him, particularly the even hotter little spot where his ogre-proportioned member was mercilessly rending mucal tissue.

He was grateful that the girls at the bathhouse had to fuck their customers on the hard steel massage tables; he had yet to find a human bed that would support the unfettered thrashings of his orgasms. They were all such delicate, matchbox contraptions.

He didn't sleep in one of them back in the shack, either. A pile of mouldering blankets and pillows formed his nest. Sentimentally attached to them, they had been scavenged from various alleys and Dumpsters upon his first arrival in this great, ugly necropolis.

The human bitch twitched beneath him; there was still a little life in her, after all. He had yet to come.

He had already been salivating when Steven Hsung ushered the evening's lineup to the reception area for his perusal. There were certain benefits to his station, he had learned.

Normally such carnal bounty went to The Mayor's Office of Mid-Town Enforcement — an arm of the borough's vice department.

But O'Farrell had an understanding with Hsung, the minor Chinatown crime lord who ran this humble, portable whorehouse that was always warned well in advance of any attempts by vice at a bust.

Hsung operated the business under the desultory camouflage of a massage parlour, and stocked it with illegal Vietnamese, Cambodian and Chinese immigrants. They had paid their life savings to be smuggled by boat into the US, and once here learned that their life savings had not been enough.

They could work off their debt with their bodies, or they could be sent back on their way across the water — without a boat.

Hsung was suspected in the murder of more than one rebellious young castaway; O'Farrell had inherited his file after the detective who had tracked the Asian pimp for the last five years retired two years before his pension to have a three-story home built in North Carolina for him and his wife.

O'Farrell, unlike Lieutenant Bill Zelinski, had little use for cash. His needs were far more basic. As it turned out, Hsung was only to happy to provide for them, since it only increased the efficiency of his organisation, anyway.

A girl on staff would start showing signs of rebellion; perhaps an attempt at going to the corner deli without one of the security boys as a chaperone, or being caught propositioning a customer to take her home and make her his girlfriend. Then it was time for a session with O'Farrell.

A session that would inevitably be her last.

A neat, and mathematically precise arrangement. Nobody fell between the cracks.

Certainly not Keiko, whose eyes had finally dried a half hour ago after she became too dehydrated to produce any more tears.

O'Farrell's method of lovemaking was not really consciously sadistic; to a fellow ogre it would have been merely enthusiastic.

But to Keiko, who was barely five feet tall and except for her long, sloping trunk had the curves of a boy, it was murder. She was bleeding from her casually mashed nose, and there were raw, bloody spots on her skull where clumps of smooth, black hair had been yanked out as easily as if they were blades of grass.

The woolly, unfragrant cheeks of the homicide detective's ass clenched, ready to help force out the come, which would be as thick as toothpaste and as scalding as fresh coffee, that now boiled in his enormous, drooping balls. Just in time, too; his knees were starting to slide wildly against the smooth steel table, as the surface had grown slick with the blood that seeped out of Keiko's other hole, already wrecked and discarded.

He put two rough, oversize thumbs against the back of Keiko's neck, ready to snap the vertebrae. The last two hours of exercise had left his stomach complaining, and he was eager to drag a side of freshly slaughtered meat down to his unmarked, where it could be stashed in the trunk for the ride to Brooklyn.

Right before he simultaneously ejaculated in Keiko's asshole and flexed his thumbs, he thought of the mystery of the shrivelled old Feeder's death, and tried to imagine what lone human could have possibly had the knowledge and ability to slay a Feeder.

Mickey O'Farrell felt an unfamiliar spear of uncertainty, enough to make him lose his terrible rhythm and release his issue at the wrong part of the thrust. Though he had already brought his fingers down and Keiko had now died anyway, it was certainly a disappointing orgasm.

X

Coming out of the bagel store carrying in her gloved hand a brown paper bag that contained a buttered bialy and a large cup of hazelnut coffee, Mary Ellen smelled smoke.

Something especially pungent was burning; sickly sweet enough to tickle her nose, trying to wheedle a sneeze out of her. Like burning taffy, maybe. Or almond, for a moment?

She stepped hesitantly down the sidewalk in the other direction from the scent, the subway stop a little less than a block away. This was the day she was to return to work, no matter how senseless and petty a course of action it seemed. There were bills to pay, if she didn't want to be turned out on the streets. And the things that waited her there now were more frightening than mere homelessness, the prospect of hunger or rape.

There were the dragon and his friends, the various creatures that made up this unpredictable new terrain, populated by a secret nation of deadly, strange predators that didn't answer to human laws of nature. Denizens of The Black.

There had been nothing in the newspapers or on TV about two bodies being found in Seven-Seventeen. Much to her concern. The tabloid press usually loved a story like that, anything that made the East Village look more weird and dangerous, and if they could malign bikers while they were at it, all the better.

But why would the cops be keeping quiet? Had she left some clue to her identity behind, fallen from her purse? A Medusa business card or a scrap of paper with a friend's phone number? Were they preparing to arrest her even now?

She didn't think so, somehow. The other logical possibility wasn't pleasant, however: that the dragon had not really been dead, and revived upon her exit. So, the cops or the dragon? Trying to imagine dealing with either prospect numbed her.

She brought the coffee to her lips, gingerly sucking at the plastic lid where it had been punctured to allow the steam to escape. Nothing more comforting on a nasty Manhattan winter's morning than hot coffee. A slightly burnt lip was actually a pleasure.

Like a good New Yorker, she had already adapted to the bad smell coming from down the block. But when the wind started to howl it was so loud and sudden she slopped a little of the blazing liquid against her mouth, scalding her dry lips.

The sound was not one she had heard before; it brought to mind a swarm of fireflies, though she knew those insects were actually silent. The wind buzzed and multiplied in the distance, it became louder even though the air on her block stayed still. She was reminded of a night when she was seven, and hauled along to the circus by her philandering father.

They had just come from the clown tent, where Father had sat with his mistress during the show, his raincoat in his lap, and his hand over that, clasping the waterproof black cotton under which a feminine hand was rooting, in his lap. When Mary Ellen had complained of boredom, he had shushed her and promised a spin on the Mad Hatter's Teacup Ride if she sat quietly like a good girl for just a few more minutes.

Then the show ended, and at last she was free, and didn't have to look at the two of them together. As they left the tent, she ran ahead.

In her little fist was a plastic bag containing three ounces of water and a goldfish that had been won for her at a game of chance. She was going to take her new pets for a ride on the Teacup.

Mary Ellen saw a lightning bug lazily floating upwards into the night air, and been momentarily distracted in her path to the ride's white picket gate.

Gaze fixed on the flashing light as it receded, little Mary Ellen hadn't seen the low-slung metal arm of the Mad Hatter's Teacup ride, painted dark and resting just a foot above the grass. She struck it with her right calf, just under the knee. Her momentum was enough that she went tumbling over, against the hard dirt.

She put her hands out in time to save her face from being scraped and muddied, but the plastic bag tore, the water quickly draining away into the dry ground. She was crying as her father grabbed her shoulders and pulled her up into his arms. Despite her sobs, he left the fish flopping there in the dark, silently choking in the air.

Several sirens jolted her from her reverie. The urgent chorus of the New York Fire Department, as red leviathan trucks raced towards some nearby disaster.

Not aware of making any decision to do so, she nevertheless found herself walking in the direction of the disturbance, as giddy and dizzy as if she had just stepped off the Mad

Hatter's Teacup Ride.

The street's morning population buzzed by on both sides of her, too intent on career advancement, or the pursuit of drugs and sex, to take the opportunity to indulge in a little anguish-sniffing voyeurism. Though the smell made her eyes water, and that weird howling — which now sounded almost human — her ears ache, her fellow New Yorkers were evidencing no such discomfort.

Turning the corner, she saw the source of the disturbance. An unkempt, abandoned tenement, probably a hundred years old, had been transformed by arson or accident into a box full of flames, tongues exploding out of broken window frames.

A crowd of half-clothed refugees were already huddled on the sidewalk. Squatters with mohawks still droopy from sleep, hastily snatched-up Doc Martens dangling from nerveless fingertips rather than adorning unwashed feet. Being watched over by a couple of beat cops who you could tell were hoping to arrest them rather than take them to the hospital.

But for one small Asian girl whose sobs cleared jaundice-coloured stripes down her blackened cheek, the squatters were a dazed, silent lot. The unearthly howls were not coming from them. Or from the cops, or the idling police cars.

The sound, and the almond odour, too, was emanating from the fire.

With a shout, the Asian girl came to life and ran toward the building's crumbling entrance. She was restrained by one of the cops.

"No! Joanne! Brigette! They're still in there!"

Mary Ellen could see by how far the flames had progressed that if Joanne and Brigette were indeed still in the building, they were no longer alive. Whatever that howling was, Mary Ellen knew it wasn't being produced by any human throat.

As she watched, the black smoke that rose from the building

became lit from within by a crackling pink-grey nimbus. The air snapped with the echo of an unheard thunderclap, and a familiar prickling sensation massaged the skin of Mary Ellen's face.

Another angel had appeared.

More huge than Haniel, it rose silently and calmly into sight as if it had been crouched behind the burning building all this time. As its great silver-blue head swivelled toward the sky, a set of infinite black wings of the same kind possessed by the other spread and kept spreading up into the winter morning sky, tips lost in the electrified black cloud, of which every billow now seemed to be a face twisted by fear and horror.

Some of the cloud's roiling drapery was lit by the angel's accompanying field of pink sparks, and the sigils on this one's chest — of a different configuration than those that adorned Haniel, Mary Ellen instinctively knew — shone luminous black.

The cop had by now cuffed the Asian girl, with the help of his fellow officer. She screamed, trying to kick and bite them, wailing her lost comrades' names in long, hoarse syllables.

One of the other squatters, a squat, muscled skinhead, bounced up and down on his feet, wanting to wade into the action but all too aware of how tightly both cops were clutching their nightsticks.

Mary Ellen could see that the boy was infected with the HIV virus, though it was presently only the dimmest glow of purple about him; previews of lesions yet to hatch.

Though the virus's ectoplasmic manifestation was disturbing, Mary Ellen felt no emanations of true evil, not like in Seven Seventeen or on the street afterward. This was only the inadvertent cruelty of biology gone awry. She felt sorry for the boy.

The fire trucks finally arrived, two of them, intersecting sirens dying down to bored purrs as their teams disembarked and went about their work in a methodical, relaxed way. Within two minutes they each had a hose trained on the blaze; Mary Ellen saw the subtle arc of a rainbow where the white flow cut through the flames. The jets of water disappeared into the looming angel's black wings, without it seeming to care or even notice.

More cops came, some riding a paddy wagon, obviously meant to scoop up the squatters. Vainly competing for passengers, an EMS truck completed the party. No one was coming out of that inferno, Mary Ellen thought.

All of the vehicles sat there, silently flashing their lights as if they were a pack of fireflies attracted to their gargantuan flaming firefly god, the god who now loomed over the burning, crumbling building, throwing off its own leviathan sparks, slowly beating its ebony wings in the exact rhythm of loss.

In truth, though, no one else could see what Mary Ellen did: The impassive angel that had come to collect its heavenly tithe, souls without bodies, now ready to be harvested. The souls, formless and stupid, little jellyfish clouds that darted about like frightened, lost children seeking their mother's hem.

This angel, who Mary Ellen abruptly knew to be called Nathaniel and Areal and Uriel — among other names — reached out a many-fingered hand, letting the two souls alight in its vibrating palm like dew or foam from the sea. On contact with the soldier of God's metallic flesh, the souls sizzled and bubbled, quickly dissolving away.

Mary Ellen found herself hating Uriel. She wondered if it would be given a successful hunter's welcome back in heaven. She assumed the gathered souls would be somehow reconstituted, once transported to whatever sort of environment could be mother to a creature such as this. To feed whatever its ruler's greater glory.

Even as the harvester of souls folded its wings and knelt back down behind the building, oblivious to the human drama it had left behind, Mary Ellen was walking away, heels beating a sharp tattoo against the pavement. There was no effect she could have on these events, and in another ten minutes she would be due at the dungeon. It wouldn't do to be late, first day back.

She was surprised at her own composure. Adapting to her new-found vision, she was finding the truth of the world an enormous weight, a burden she wasn't quite sure how to shoulder. But still, she felt herself pushed on by some more resolute heart than her own, against her own will, playing perhaps on her fear of death, or of damnation. A concept she hadn't taken seriously in decades, since pubescence, at least. Loss of sexual innocence had brought loss of faith, just like the nuns warned. And she had been glad they were right.

The brisk Chelsea air bit her cheeks, and the light down in the canyons of Sixth Avenue was clear and still, despite the bustling morning traffic on both street and sidewalk. An elaborate structure of wood and iron piping stood above a steaming eruption in the pavement, fluorescent flags showing the way safely around.

The steam was silent and heavy, another proof of elements transmuting, energy evolving, species that could manifest themselves on multiple planes of existence. Everything changed, according to invisible plans. God and Nature did not communicate with such baser races as humans, to make their intentions known. She had never thought to believe in God again. She wasn't sure she was altogether too pleased by the development, either.

Mary Ellen became aware of her portable breakfast, still clutched in her hands. Sipping at the considerably cooled coffee, she decided to see what would happen if she just worried about the rent, and tried to stay out of the way of angels, dragons, zombies and God.

There are times, she thought, when denial can be a good thing.

XI

*t*wo weeks later, Mary Ellen was not achieving anything like the return to normalcy for which she had hoped. Although Mistress Medusa's reappearance on the dungeon schedule was enthusiastically greeted by several pining clients, as well as the more friendly, less competitive of the mistresses, the actual resumption of duties did not go altogether smoothly.

The unpredictable input of her new senses was a recurring distraction, a source of surprise, shock and frequent disgust. After three days and five sessions, though, Mary Ellen had some hope that she was going to be able to cope.

But there had been so much to learn, so many conclusions to be drawn from the data collected, and with no instructor save her own intuition and logic. A constant series of tests, and some of them…she could particularly have done without the discovery that the guilty oozed that gross ectoplasmic pus.

But now, she was having to deal with a more immediate,

plebeian problem than ectoplasm seeping up at her from the wounds she was paid to inflict.

She was facing The Manager.

Clad in one of his many black flight suits, zipped down his chest to reveal a huge, biomechanical tattoo, he was hobbling around on his one good leg in his trademark state of relaxed agitation.

"Having been in the domination business longer than many of those girls out there have been having their periods, Mary Ellen, I've seen all sorts of situations develop, so many cases of good people suffering from burnout, that it makes me sad. It makes me want to help them."

As unpleasant as the prospect seemed to her, he was happy with the challenge of helping Mary Ellen with her 'situation', as he had a few moments ago so authoritatively defined the stray mishaps of the last few days.

"You've been a real asset to this place, you know. I waited for you to come here a long time, I knew you'd get a raw deal at the other dungeons."

'Condition' was another word he wielded. One of the other girls had already warned Mary Ellen about that one, revealing how their employer was entertaining his nightly array of special guests with the mysterious, fascinating tale of Mistress Medusa's nervous breakdown and evident self-mutilation attempt on Christmas Eve.

"I'd like to think I'm a better boss than those people, and that's why you're here."

Mary Ellen knew that his intentions weren't even deliberately harmful; when the drugs were interacting in his busy bloodstream in exactly the right manner, The Manager's innate humanity could actually emerge in the most unsuspected ways. He was the sort who would actively campaign among his regular clients on behalf of his older, less-desirable mistresses, and confer some of the house's profits on employees who had been suffering too many slow days.

"You need money, someone to talk to? Come to me."

He was just as likely, though, to "forget" to pay you for your credit card receipts, or, if in a truly unmedicated mood, fine you for being late to your shift.

"I just want you to know that we're all behind you, Mary Ellen. Maybe you think you don't have friends here, but you do."

Mary Ellen smiled nervously. She hated it when The Manager got fatherly.

"Take Mistress Olivia, for example."

"That *bitch* — " Mary Ellen blurted, damning herself for giving him encouragement.

"Now, I know you hate her, and you two have had some sort of competition thing going on..."

Mary Ellen didn't feel the need to compete with Mistress Olivia. She was a stealing, lying bitch, a smart-ass little Mexican-American Princess who had once stolen her favourite slave away to be her boyfriend. And promptly done the schmuck more physical damage than she ever had. She felt the need to smack Mistress Olivia upside the well-coiffured head.

"But a bunch of us were talking, well, about you, and your experience, and she was the first one to say that we should keep you on shift, because now was when you really needed everybody to stand behind you and help you get back on your feet."

"I don't think Olivia knows a lot about being on her feet. I don't think she spends much time there," Mary Ellen sedately remarked.

"Now, I have a two o'clock coming in any minute, who always takes a three-hour. He likes me in a businesswoman's outfit, however. May I get ready, please?"

Collapsing back on his bed, his hand already moving toward

his stash, The Manager appeared pained by Mary Ellen's lack of co-operation, depriving him the pleasure of lavishing pity.

She turned from him. The familiarity of her ire was actually comforting; The Manager, at least, could be managed, and by conventional means. She no longer thought of him as any sort of monster at all, now that she had met real ones.

There were no monsters here. Maybe The Black wasn't everywhere. Maybe it passed through places, like a fever or a virus.

The thing that had visite′ ie dungeons, though terrifying, had not been from The 1 .ack. More and more, Mary Ellen found herself speculating if it could have been a manifestation of God, or of his invisible dominions. If God could indeed be so inhuman, sadistic and oblique, so casually punishing.

Whatever it was, though, the dungeon manifestation had swept through, and back into oblivion. Since that night, Mary Ellen, despite her initial fears to the contrary, could detect nothing of the otherworldly about any of the rooms, or any of the diverse stream of clients who trudged up the two sets of stairs to the parlour.

It was true, that her perception of the latter had changed. Mary Ellen's new vision illuminated the furtive, surly, clingy, arrogant, suicidal nature of the lawyers, doctors, students, professional athletes, firemen, cops, drug dealers and insurance agents that paid by the hour to drain the pus from their psychic wounds.

Mary Ellen had been disgusted beyond words the first time she saw *that*. A chubby, sleek personal injury lawyer strode out of Dungeon Two behind Lady North, the knot of his striped tie still between his fingers.

His stained fingers. Ochre-stained. As she realised when she later saw it weep from another client's — a real estate speculator's — caning bruises, it was the signature hue of psychic poison. The stuff also bore a powerfully sweet stink, something like burnt almonds but with a lurking shadow of rot. The same as the tormented souls burnt to death in the fire.

In fact, Mary Ellen detected that odour now, approaching her, already heavy in the air as it drifted across the threshold of the Manager's doorway.

The cloud stunk like a business luncheon attended by all of her most twisted clients, with maybe a couple of junkies and AIDS cases thrown in for good measure.

No longer so eager to be rid of The Manager's company, Mary Ellen, paused, and murmured to herself, lips moving but no sound escaping. She felt her nose wrinkle.

A throaty, musical voice came from around the corner, ending a declaration directed toward the living room in a light bark of laughter.

Mary Ellen cocked her head, hearing a strange Doppler effect in the sound, a vague sort of electrical interference.

"Oh, Medusa, I forgot to tell you," The Manager spoke up from behind her. "We brought a new girl on board while you were out. This is the first time you've both been on the same shift."

A grinning demon appeared in the doorway. Conquering her fear, Mary Ellen had to admit that by this time it was almost an expected sight.

XII

Lady Calie slit the seal on a fresh package of surgical sutures as she regarded the challenges presented by the mysterious and odd Mistress Medusa.

"Observe your fate, you fool, shrink-wrapped for your protection," she announced archly and on schedule, eliciting an enthusiastic moan from her client. It had better be enthusiastic; she expected more than mere money for her time and attention, even if the latter were splintered.

She had gone back to The Manager's office to inform him her client had requested a second dominatrix join his session. The Manager's policy demanded that any such change in the fee schedule be cleared through him, so that none of the girls could bring each other in for extra money without him getting his required percentage. They did it anyway, of course; girls will be girls.

Calie, however, was not interested in cheating for nickels and dimes. Therefore, she had been on her way to his stuffy office and studio apartment in the rear when she ran straight into the most intriguing human she had met for a hundred years — a mortal who could actually see her.

Somewhat amused, somewhat alarmed, she had immediately tried to recruit the woman for her session, even though she had been about to suggest to The Manager that she utilise Lady Marlena, who was a stupid girl but at least not a distraction to Calie's art.

"Just a few thin little strands of thread, a little sewing lesson, a bit of tactile information to process. You can do it, can't you?"

But Medusa had balked at the offer. The pale, distracted brunette with the striking blue eyes radiated confusion and mistrust towards Calie. It was almost as if she understood her fellow domina's true nature. Which was impossible, of course.

So desirable had Medusa been, more so for the facile begging off, claiming she needed extra time to prepare for her upcoming two o'clock. Calie had wryly noted that The Manager's bland, schoolroom wall clock showed it to be only twelve-thirty; no session at a dungeon like this took that much preparation.

Despite The Manager's obvious displeasure at losing his percentage, this Mistress Medusa had held her ground, however. Quietly defiant, she had betrayed her distrust for Calie when she pretended not to notice the outstretched hand of the other mistress as Calie expressed her regrets and hopes that they could work together in the future, and wasn't this dungeon the absolute best in the city and a wonderful place to work?

Medusa had merely smiled wryly and murmured, "Used to be. It's getting a little weird lately."

Thoroughly provoked, Calie had returned to the living room, making a desultory pick-up of the delighted Lady Marlena as she went.

"Mistress? Would you mind fetching the Betadine and a few

blotting pads? This will be a messy operation," Calie now asked her pale second choice for co-conspirator.

Lady Marlena was a vague, pot and ecstasy-stung young lesbian from California who wore a straw-coloured wig over her shaved head and had four rings in each of her labia.

"Yes, Mistress Calie," she lisped, smiling nervously as she squatted before the ornate, knee-high cherry wood cabinet where Dungeon One's medical supplies were kept.

Observing the pleasant way the woman's ass strained her leather g-string and fishnets, Calie thought again of the older but equally lush creature she had just met in The Manager's office. And was surprised at herself, to be so captivated.

But what a welcome diversion, this new puzzle! She wished Medusa had come in on this session; it would be a bloody one. She'd have liked to have gauged the woman's reaction.

"Now, pincushion, we begin our lesson," Calie said, nodding for Marlena to tip the bottle over their captive's chest. Twin dark orange runnels ran down his chest and met in his crotch.

Normally, Calie hated two-mistress sessions; having no interest in the petty competitiveness, the crass and childish power plays most of these empty-headed young girls committed to try and win a twenty-dollar tip.

Money was of laughable concern; cash was always available when needed. A series of bank accounts throughout the Americas, the Philippines and India guaranteed that. She simply couldn't stand the crass greed and petty insolence of these little girls.

She took the pre-threaded needle to moist, clean flesh, quickly and professionally sliding it beneath and out, pull, beneath and out, pull. Her client moaned. She looked up into his dilated eyes.

"Pardon me, did you say something?"

He shook his head emphatically no. Lady Marlena giggled.

Lady Calie was used to tribute, and not just of the niggardly sort these dungeon clients so begrudgingly offered, clutching their gold cards and fresh hundred dollar bills. Most of these wretched men were hardly interested in true subservience and sacrifice; they sought the absolution of a goddess. Smug creatures, they thought it could be paid for with silly pieces of green paper.

But this goddess had been spoiled by too many rare gifts. The hearts of an entire village's first-borns, left in a great stone chalice on the windy peak of a Mayan pyramid, served to her as she reclined on a throne chiselled from the fused bones of several hundred years worth of slow-witted Christian missionaries.

An anguished groan escaped the client. Not spirited enough for her taste.

After passing her latexed palm across the client's forehead, slightly stunning him so that he wouldn't squirm or bleat again, Calie began to sew in earnest, moving with inhuman swiftness. As her design took shape — a cradle of surgical thread latticing across her client's shaved-smooth chest — she fell further into thought.

"Ooh, that's beautiful, mistress," Lady Marlena squeaked from over her shoulder. Calie grimaced in reply, irritated at the distraction. Not from the sewing; that she could have done with her eyes shut. And had, more than once before, just for the mild fun of it.

She was still thinking about the woman in The Manager's office.

On the surface, Medusa seemed a fairly unremarkable example of a second- or third-generation urban Western female. There was a wet gleam in those blue eyes that suggested a not uncommon degree of neurotic hysteria.

If her condition seemed to parade itself in a more enticingly brittle way than in many of the similar women Calie had taken for lovers and food during her tenure in this still young land, it was because hysteria flourished in such volatile proximity to the magnesium vapours of hunger and aggression that she had seen seeping up from Medusa's pale flesh.

Evidence of a sex ka boiling like tar in the bitch's belly.

Just the sort of food that could still tempt a 1000-year old demon of the flesh into wonderfully fiendish lengths of seduction. Oh, yes, to feel like a whelp again!

But there was more to Medusa than her delectability, Calie knew. Consider her rare gift of second sight, an ability usually brought on by a brush with the infinite. Could that incident also be the inspiration for her hysteria, then?

Calie had a clue about that: how fearsome and provocative was the brief moment she thought she saw protective sigils that only the fingers of the eternal could had painted, glowing upon Mistress Medusa's cheeks and forehead.

For a human to receive such a communion was rare, at least during the last several hundred years. But if so, then no wonder Medusa was so jumpy, so removed and unsure — even in her interactions with The Manager, a brooding old junkie who these predatory human girls had all learned soon enough how to manipulate.

From the way Medusa kept staring at her while The Manager nattered on in his usual dazed chatter about the similarities between the two of them, and how the session would be a great chance to get to know each other, Calie speculated that Medusa had indeed been granted a sliver of the unnameable enemy's infallible sight. Which would make her as uncommon among humanity as Calie was among all the diverse Feeder races, no matter what the era.

"Could you hold this down while I tie that," Calie asked Lady Marlena, who set aside the brown bottle and cotton pads to put a latex-covered finger where the domina's nod indicated. The cradle was complete. A slight moan, muffled by layers of leather and nylon, issued from two feet above.

"Now, George, I don't want any back talk from you," Calie joked, and reached up to yank the fishing line attached to the rubber-tipped clamps screwed tightly on to the client's stretched nipples. His head snapped back in agony, but no more sound issued from within the slightly baggy leather hood. It was a house toy, not the client's custom accessory. Very stylish.

Oh, the things that preoccupied humans; they effectively distracted themselves even when they had stumbled on the road to a slightly higher plane. Sometimes she felt a maternal kinship with them. If only they all weren't so stupid.

The loneliness that engulfed Calie in her first five hundred years of existence had finally given way to exultation over her unique origins. She was an impossible crossbreeding of not only species but competing Natures themselves; part immortal, part Feeder.

Sometimes she even suspected there was an unlikely trace of angel's blood within her; an infeasible lineage, since the hermaphrodite soldiers of God were not known to be capable of reproduction. Maybe angelic rape, some high-handed act of holy vengeance perpetrated against one of her great grandmothers; a shape-shifter or a blood-drinker who became too greedy or hunted in the wrong place at the wrong time and became an example.

Feeding on the singular likes of Medusa could bring down just such a judgement on her own head. Though Calie was indeed bored with existence, she didn't believe that she had as of yet begun to entertain a suicide wish. At least as far as she could tell.

But *wouldn't* it be a great and sly smite at the smug All Powerful, to give His rare toy over to a slavering mob of

Feeders? There were many base and squirming races that would gladly consume the husk that would be left after Calie took her sweet share, that most ephemeral yet filling part of a human.

The soul. The fear. The love. The belief. Each so beautiful in its singular identity, even more when it was just a fading memory, a residue of dark energy dissolving in her belly.

"Now, George, let's really turn you into a piece of artwork. Would you like to be a performance artist for a day, George?"

Lady Marlena's brainless giggle made an encore, while George issued a grunt of uncertainty from behind the featureless hood. Trembling knees betrayed his concern.

"Marlena, will you calm our performer? He seems to be nervous."

Lady Marlena smiled; unlike some of the girls, she had no problem with handling the client's penises in a gentle way. She had worked at two massage parlours before coming here. She began stroking his small cock, which quickly sprung perpendicular with the attention, the slit pointed at Calie like a blind, brainless eye.

Retrieving a piece of the silver wrapping paper she had left on the bondage table at the beginning of the session, Calie casually folded it into the shape of a cartoon heart; not the real organ, which she intimately knew the taste and smell of, but the benign, haunch-shaped icon the humans had adopted, rather than confront nature in all its bloody wonder.

"That's beautiful, Mistress Calie," exclaimed Marlena, batting her eyes flirtatiously while she continued to lightly milk George's cock.

"Do you like it, George?" Calie smirked, as she tucked it in the cradle of surgical thread that adorned the bound man's breast. He nodded, lost in the pleasure of his handjob, glad that Lady Calie had brought in such a generous mistress to the session.

Just so Lady Marlena wouldn't be confused, Calie made a

great show of palming a box of wooden matches, extracting one and holding it up to the light. George shook his head, and you could see the whites of his eyes even past the folds of the hood's eye holes.

"Yes, yes, yes. Suffer for your art, George. It has to come from the heart, you know," Calie purred, and struck the match.

When she touched the silver heart, however, it was not the match but the heat of her own fingers which caused the paper to burst into flames.

Lady Marlena applauded, giggling in delight. Calie inhaled the slight odour of singing flesh deeply, and imagined drinking the blood from Medusa's punctured breast.

XIII

*t*hings moved in the club's shadows. An awkward, thin
man, his face contorted with passion, swung upside
down on a rope a few feet above the stage.

His long, jutting limbs were twined around the thick cord,
microphone clutched between the fingers of his claw-like left
hand, windscreen nearly engulfed by a mouth drawn back in
the rictus of an angry hiss from the back of his throat, a martial melody executed in tones of cut glass, rafting along the
tide of bone-rattling bass, while somewhere in the background guitars bled the static of a hundred blank radio bands.

His black hair hung straight down from his scalp; his pointed jaw jabbed the air as he let loose with a scream that raked
the audience's ears. One burly, unshaven leather jacket owner
actually tapped the side of his skull, as if some ancient block-
age had finally been dissolved.

Mary Ellen felt the intimacy of the Black, languorously
coagulated in the shadows infesting the maze of narrow pas-

sageways at the back of the club. The grotto had been provided by the management for the less exhibitionistic to seek their hurried and perverse sex under a dimmer blanket, away from the stage area.

She tried to sense if anyone, or anything, roamed those corridors, where reddened flesh welted in crude glyphs and orgasm's seed languished in the cruel set of a full mouth. The maze would be a perfect banquet hall for Feeders, a ready-made mausoleum for any unfortunate lured in by their shadowy promise.

Two weeks had passed since Axel's death, and no one had come after her. Not the authorities, nor any more monsters. Lady Calie was terrifying, there was no doubt about that. But the small, foreign mistress had made no threatening moves. The way she looked at Mary Ellen, however, as if she wanted her bound and naked on a huge plate, was nerve-wracking.

Mary Ellen had spent the first few weeks since the apocalyptic confrontation in the biker bar waiting to be arrested, or perhaps murdered and bones sucked clean in vengeance.

Instead, another of her closely-held notions of the nature of existence had simply melted away; you *could* kill somebody and get away with it. In a public bathroom, even.

The realisation helped fuel her growing alienation from everything around her. She had explained to her slave Billy, slowly, patiently, that the contract they had signed together in his blood was no longer valid, because she was no longer the same mistress he had come on his knees to, seeking the safety of ownership.

She had thought about keeping him just for protection, even having him move in her apartment, but after much debate decided that he would be nearly as helpless as she against the sort of creature that had attacked her in Seven Seventeen.

Besides, her patience had run short with the vague molasses that Billy, and most everyone else, for that matter, seemed happy to drown in.

They worried about stupid matters like rent and taxes and relationships, when more than one world around them was crackling with black and blinding energies, pyrotechnical clues of some eternal, a vein of once unsolvable secrets now partially exposed and waiting to unfold, sweeping and sensuous.

These were the secrets that lurked underneath every Sunday School lesson, every science class, every college seminar on world religion. Gods and monsters and immortality. Myth and superstition revealed to be a part of her world. The rational, quantifiable natural realm had suddenly seen its boundaries stretched so far that she felt like Christmas Eve had been the true moment of virginity lost, or perhaps even of birth.

But with her exultation at this new knowledge came both grief and fear. Why was *she* out of all souls saddled with the vision to recognise such horrors? This was her new world, and there was no going back to the cocoon of innocence she had once been safely encased in. Or the people she had loved, hated or needed there. She still lived among them, but was not truly with them anymore.

Every waking moment, and all of her dreams, were filled with a near-constant sense of alarm, an urgency. She felt the need to seek some sort of help, a strength or at least an explanation, outside of what she could muster. But where could she possibly go? The only place she had ever found an inkling of this shadow world with its nefarious population was in luridly written paperback novels.

Every night for the past two weeks, she had lay in bed staring up at the ceiling, its cracks and impurities thrown into sharp detail by the lamp she now needed lit to lull her into slumber, hoping she would see in its abstract the answer to who might help her, who might *know*.

She had thought of the clergy, but passed on that idea. They would refer her to a psychiatrist, most likely. The various ministers and rabbis she had come into contact with since her childhood were a down-to-earth lot, more concerned about the financial status of their respective churches, fed by the fealty of their flocks.

No longer amused by the blaring music or the singer hanging upside down, Mary Ellen headed for the bar, passing a plain-looking woman who wore a nun's wimple but not the robe; her body was clad only in leather bra and garter belt. A fat, middle-aged man cowered at her heels, back crossed with the marks left by the silver-tongued whip gripped in her right hand.

Right. The Catholic rituals were lousy with mysticism, it was true, but as far as she could tell, the priests who carried them out viewed them as metaphors – gentle or powerful poetry meant to open the mind. Miracles were few and far between by their reasoning, and Satan was an amorphous concept; to them, Evil's only worldly agents were the abortionists and pornographers, or those in the government or fourth estate who sought to investigate the finer points of the necessary profit structure required for the Church to survive.

Slipping into a seat at the bar, she signalled the keep, a dour lesbian with a lavishly long ponytail. The woman nodded, not yet finished serving a well-muscled gay man dressed as a state trooper.

The police, of course, were out of the question. They had never been anything but a threat to her and her various friends; bikers and rock 'n' rollers and drug dealers and sex workers. The police had been useless when she'd been mugged and groped in the East Village when she was twenty, and they would be useless now.

"Vodka and cranberry juice," she shouted in the bartender's ear, smelling the residue of a bland, manly soap.

What was left? The government, the press? They were notorious rationalists; the only bogeymen the FBI acknowledged were Middle Eastern terrorists and right-wing survivalist militias.

And by the evidence of the newspapers she infrequently read, reporters these days found Mystery only in the tawdry drug and sex-soaked antics of politicians and celebrities; they did not even try to expose any hoaxes that suggested the existence of the supernatural; they merely ridiculed or ignored them, throwing them on the crackpot heap. They'd find a place for her there, too.

Of course, there were the more pagan religions, it was true – fingers of an older time that tenuously touched the New World by way of New York City's constantly mutating stream of immigrants.

Her drink came; the lesbian waved away her five-dollar bill. Mary Ellen felt a surge of embarrassment; had word of her 'breakdown' spread to here? The Manager was overly talkative when he was high, and he often came rambling into this club after the dungeon closed on Saturday nights.

She knew of the outlaw religions vaguely, from the occasional Sunday supplement article on the voodoo queens of Harlem, and the Santeria cults of the Lower East Side.

But she feared that those cynical reporters were right in this case, that they were charlatans preying on the uneducated; power-mongers who would welcome a superstitious middle-class white woman into their parlours only so they could pick her wallet.

The implacable assault of the industrial music mocked her, grabbed her nervous system and stroked it with a rough, uncaring thumb, heightening her uneasiness. A lyric jumped out at her: *"I've got to find my hole, I've got to burn you down."* It was as if the music were lashing her, demanding an immediate solution to her situation.

A cheap-looking young woman strode by. She looked like a

mixture of Hispanic and Black, nice body if you overlooked that her pelvic girdle was a bit over-padded. Pretty but feral face, narrow eyes and dark hair in tight, frizzy curls. Nothing on but a black lace body suit and a pair of inexpensive thigh-highs.

Mary Ellen snorted to herself; probably a pro at one of the handjob palaces, where the greasy owners turned the other way if the mistresses wanted to earn a better tip at the end of the session, by applying a little spit and muscle to coax forth the client's complete satisfaction.

Three men were caught up in the girl's wake, all desperately trying to look as if they were meandering, rather than pathetically trotting after her like sheep. Slobs, with glasses and clumsily-styled facial hair. One was even wearing corduroy pants. *How do they find their way to clubs like this,* Mary Ellen wondered?

The song ended, and Mary Ellen felt a moment of free fall, a blessed absence of assault which spiralled down into relief as she welcomed back a relative sense of well-being.

Without a word of farewell, the singer, who had let go of the rope and finished his screams of self-righteous protest against the ennui of existence prone on his belly, now stalked off the stage, radiating studied awareness of his own mean, bitter elegance.

The great speakers on either side of the stage clicked and hummed for a moment, as the prerecorded accompaniment was damped, and the line switched over to the house DJ, who surveyed his realm from an aerie high in the far western corner of the club, right behind an iron rafter.

"Thank you so much, Mr. Happy Boots. And for our next trick, we're going to pull a rabbit out of your ass. Drink up, everybody, the club closes in half an hour. Drink up...whatever it is you're drinking. Hope you're playing safe."

Canned music came on, old '80s New Wave disco stuff, at a less punishing volume. Mary Ellen started when she heard a woman's voice next to her ear.

"Medusa, dear. How are you doing, poor thing? I haven't seen you here in weeks," a feminine voice said softly. Mary Ellen felt its owner's breath on her ear.

Mary Ellen spun on her stool, and was immediately surprised by a new perspective on a once-familiar colleague. She answered back politely.

"Hello, Juliette. I've been busy."

"It's nice to see you back among the living," Juliette replied. Among the living. The living? Mary Ellen stared in wonderment at the other domina.

The Manager complained about Juliette all the time. She ran a lavish dungeon a dozen blocks away from his, that on occasion attracted his more elite clients.

Mary Ellen wondered what The Manager would say if he could see that his competitor wasn't really a woman. Female, yes, but not human. Beneath a translucent paper of dead flesh, she was a creature made out of black flames which flickered violently yet threw no heat. Mary Ellen shuddered.

"Oh dear, it *is* drafty in here, isn't it?" Juliette commiserated, a wicked smile curling her European lips.

Weariness, hurt and hatred emanated from the shade, the inconsolable loneliness of the once human. Mary Ellen realised Juliette was of this thing that she called The Black, an abstract name for a portion of existence that lurked beneath humanity like an opaque pool, leviathan tentacles hungrily breaking the surface once in a while, each an implacable hunter.

But rather than feel threatened by proximity to her fellow mistress, she felt merely removed and guarded. She sensed that she was safe from Juliette's hungers, whether they were for blood or for human power.

Ghostly black fingers seeped from Juliette's pores, and, more grossly still, from every available orifice, moving over Mary

Ellen in a manner that betrayed curiosity rather than hostility.

When they actually touched flesh she was struck by a fresh bout of chills, cut short when some sort of static electricity charge burst in her ears and the fingers went streaming back into their mother.

Juliette stiffened for a moment, her thick eyebrows drawn sharply down over narrowed eye slits. Then she relaxed. Shaking her head, she laughed.

"So *that's* the way it is… Mary Ellen, dear, could I trouble you to deliver a message for me?"

"To whom?"

Mary Ellen expected her to name The Manager. The rivalry between the two of them was ongoing; The Manager constantly announced suspicions that Juliette was scouting for employees among his staff.

"A message to your special client. The Christmas Eve legend. The one who made you like this, poor saint."

"Pardon me, but I don't know what the hell you're talking about."

The bitterness of the lie made Mary Ellen's tongue numb and clumsy. Juliette merely nodded condescendingly.

"Just humour an old, old mistress, sweet. Tell the One who made you that a Lorsange never forgives or forgets."

"If you mean The Manager, I'll give him the message."

Juliette put a black-light hand lightly on Mary Ellen's arm, fingertips prickly with static electricity.

"Medusa, I have no hatred for you. To be a pawn is to be just as ill-used, as cursed, as I was, and still am. Peace for us all will come some day, I promise, through the toppling of this merciless order."

Mary Ellen was trying to formulate a reply to Juliette's riddles when they were joined by Alexis and Candida, another pair of dominas that worked for The Manager.

"Hello, fellow mistresses," intoned Alexis, a short, extravagantly clothed woman who was of some peasant Eurasian extraction, her features half way between the beautiful and the simian. Her right eyebrow was pierced twice with gold rings, and her eyes danced with a disarming gleam of self-mockery.

Mary Ellen was grateful for the intrusion; these women were at least human. Whatever their character flaws.

"Ladies, next week is the Black Ball, and as professional sex workers, you are both invited to be honoured guests," Alexis announced with a flourish, as Candida, a tall, fair-skinned Amazon, took her cue to hand them expensively-printed invitations.

"How nice," Juliette replied, scanning the card. "Oh, look, though, it's on Friday. I have a special client I'm travelling to meet in Los Angeles this weekend. Sorry, ladies, I'll have to wait for all the gossip. I'm sure it'll be juicy. You won't let me down, will you, Medusa?"

Mary Ellen smiled, taking the offered refuge in the familiar, catty interactions of her particular strata of Manhattan society.

"No, of course not, Juliette. All the gory stuff. Thank you for the invitation, ladies."

"No, thank *you*," Alexis said, starting the sentence in a purr but ending it in a drawl.

The Manager had a bit of a crush on Alexis, Mary Ellen suspected. He probably wouldn't if he knew the way the sly, diminutive beauty skimmed cash off sessions and encouraged the other mistresses to do it, too.

The arch social manoeuvrings were presently interrupted by a sharp cry of pain from the stage.

"Athena's at it again," Alexis wryly exclaimed.

Under an ice-blue spotlight a tall, willowy redhead was savagely kicking a supine man in his belly. Compact and stocky, he wore leather jacket and jockstrap, and was curled like a caterpillar on the axis that began at the woman's leather-shod toe.

Mistress Athena braced herself against a leather-padded gymnast's horse, her long, straight hair dangling in her oval face, nearly obscuring the distant, hostile glint of her violet eyes. She was clad in a violet-hued latex mini dress that high-lighted her taut, long curves.

"I think they call it edge play," Candida offered. It was rare for her to speak in public.

"I think I call it a mugging," Alexis rejoined, chuckling.

"I think I want a closer look," Mary Ellen said to no one in particular, making an excuse to move away, closer to the stage. It was brighter there, and Athena's infamously vicious style of mistressing didn't disturb her in the least.

She recognised the man being kicked. Mercurio, a female-to-male sex change who, after attaching himself to several lifestyle mistresses in town, had finally settled on Athena, whose sense of drama matched his own.

Mary Ellen had seen him display his dick here at the club. A strip of flesh peeled off his belly and rolled into a cylinder, a flap of skin mottled with sprouts of displaced pubic hair that could only be made stiff by the insertion of a six-inch surgical steed rod. Mercurio had demonstrated, on his Mistress's command.

At this moment, however, Mercurio's mistress had taken to jumping up and down on her slave's stomach, high heels land-ing sharply in his sternum. Several more sensitive-souls from the gathered audience shook their heads and retreated. There were other professional mistresses among the contingent.

Regardless, Mercurio seemed unperturbed, allowing no evi-dence he felt the impact other than a slight curling of his nar-row fingers, folding in just short of making a fist. His mouth was not open; if the wind was being forced from him, you couldn't hear it over the DJ's techno-industrial mix.

Athena signalled the end of the scene by brusquely stalking

away, ignoring Mercurio. He was left to recover and follow her to the bar when he was able.

As various knots of club goers now drifted back and forth, seeking the next attraction, Mary Ellen noted Alexis closing in on her again. Rather than subject herself to more cat and mouse deviousness, she intercepted Athena.

"That was quite a startling exhibition, Mistress," Mary Ellen admired.

"Why, thank you. He's been an awful slave all week, off brooding and drinking when he's supposed to be running errands. Sometimes just disciplining him is a full time job," Athena replied. A warm smile spread across what until this moment had been blank features, lost somewhere in the faraway.

Athena was notorious among the atheists of the New York scene for her spiritual beliefs. A New Age adherent, she dwelled in a posh downtown apartment, a cavern of crystals and pyramids. From this base she managed not only her domination business but also the Alga Foundation, a modest cult in miniature that featured her as the goddess at its centre. She reigned over a flock variously made up of the impressionable, the unorthodox and, of course, the curious and horny.

A striking beauty, lit from inside by the barely suppressed glow of madness. Since her childhood, Athena had claimed a second sight… at least according to the stories The Manager had told Mary Ellen when against her better judgement she had spent some time between clients with the party crowd in the dungeon's back room.

"She was afraid to sit in the chair in the corner of her bedroom when she was five, because a demon lived under it who would whisper dirty things to her," The Manager explained once between toots.

"That demon also, she claimed, told her the exact date her father would die. And two years later, he did," The Manager finished the story with a flourish, offering Mary Ellen a rolled-up hundred and a line.

"Athena, I wonder if you could help me with an, um, spiritual matter," Mary Ellen ventured, following an impulse.

Athena immediately brightened even further. She moved closer in a manner that would have been sisterly had she not run her nails lightly across Mary Ellen's fishnet-covered thigh, almost snagging the weave.

"I knew there was something different about you from the last time we met. You've had your eyes opened, haven't you?"

Mary Ellen grimaced.

"I guess that's one way to describe it. I don't know how to quite explain what's happened, really, or what to do about it. I know you've studied a lot of esoteric areas, and you have the foundation — "

"Come to my home. Tonight," Athena insisted, grabbing Mary Ellen's bicep and stroking it with a long, patrician thumb.

"The stars are in special places tonight. There's no time like now to confront the future. Your future."

They were joined by Mercurio, already bearing his mistress's long, green velvet coat. Greased black hair fell across his burning gaze, which was kept cast floorwards but for a bare moment in which he glanced suspiciously at Mary Ellen. Wondering what influence his capricious, wilful goddess was allowing into her home *now*.

XIV

"*Mother of the Inferno, we beseech you; obsidian butterfly, bless our souls; goddess of filth and degeneration, we call upon your pure mercy.*"

Athena's back was arched, her long, nude white figure tightly drawn so that her shocking pink nipples, perpetually vulnerable and new-looking, aimed out the open window, towards some distant, impassive constellation of stars.

Her long, crimson hair fell back like a gout of blood from her oval, patrician features. The allure of inbreeding among the noble.

Mercurio and Marina, her bookended slaves, observed raptly, gazes silvery with devotion to their goddess and mistress. In the background, a huge home entertainment complex spun a backdrop, the large TV screen displaying a series of empty desert landscapes and cleansing midnight fires while the stereo piped-in a minimalist instrumental piece, the sound of metal drawn against metal.

Mercurio, the female-to-male sex change, had been a brooding lesbian claiming the classic psycho-malaise of being a man trapped in a woman's body.

Now he was something at least roughly male, sewn together with luxurious scars at the breasts and crotch, the rest of his flesh covered with a crazy maze of impulsive tattooing, much of it done by his own untrained hand.

Crouched in worn Levi's and shirtless before his mistress, Mercurio brooded still; a study in extreme alienation. Perhaps because the transformation hadn't been everything he had expected, perhaps because it was simply in his nature.

Marina was Mercurio's counterpart in almost every way. A hulking, muscular man bumping down the shadowy corridor to femininity, he was squeezed into a black body suit and padded bra, a silver ankh dangling in his false cleavage. His complexion was craggy from depilation and the female hormones he shot. His hair, though long, was still as dull and thin as that of any middle-aged man.

Mary Ellen knew that where Mercurio was too much trouble to be a practical prize, Marina was a true servant to his mistress's cause. Self-employed as a computer program troubleshooter, he sat at his terminal adorned in earrings and lipstick, seeking to spend as much of his life as possible parroting the rough image of the feminine he worshipped in all women, but Athena in particular.

He calculated Athena's taxes, cooked and cleaned, and was setting her up with a Web site on the Internet. That was the new frontier for clients, some mistresses thought. The easy sort of client, who spent too much time at the keyboard, who collected the most money for their labours in the shortest amount of time and, due to the unworldliness that was a side effect of their secluded labours, had not the first idea how to spend it.

Which is where quite a few of the mistresses Mary Ellen knew were only too happy to provide firm and loving guidance.

Athena was different in that respect. She seemed fond of money, all right, enjoying its ostentations and comforts. But she was what The Manager liked to refer to as a "lifestyle mistress," a woman who dominated those around here because it was simply her nature, and practised her crafts whether she was being paid or not.

The Manager respected lifestyle mistresses, but often seemed hard-pressed to keep them on staff. There was something about all the drug traffic and teenage runaways coming around, the spotty management style, that dampened their enthusiasm for the dungeon, though it was undeniably a physically beautiful arena.

Athena was a sight of corporeal splendour at the moment, too. Mary Ellen tried to ride with the abstract pleasure of watching the woman's sweeping dance before the open window's pale moon, and not grind the back of her teeth with worry that she was wasting precious time here, that there was no way this would solve her problems.

Well, there were no better ideas occurring to her at the moment. Axel had seemed like a much more solid bet, a no-nonsense bad customer with a famously tough peer group. Look what had happened there.

Mary Ellen resisted the urge to reach over to her purse, four feet away by the foot of a pushed-aside coffee table, so she could dip her hand inside and feel the faint comfort of the murdered biker's iron dagger. When she was out, she usually performed that nervous gesture every half hour or so, but here in Athena's apartment she felt self-conscious. Marina turned toward her and smiled comfortingly, aware of her anxiousness.

"My mistress is very educated. She's seen and done some amazing things," Marina whispered hoarsely.

Amazing? Even you wouldn't believe it, Mary Ellen thought, tightening her lips in perfunctory response.

The music was reaching a slowly building crescendo, the metallic scrapes now long and provocatively ragged. From the shelf of an antique sideboard Athena retrieved both a purple leather cat-of-nine-tails and a foot-long, multi-faceted crystal rod. She swayed over to Mary Ellen and gently laid the point of the crystal against the sitting woman's forehead. Athena spoke back over her shoulder, to the flat moon in the window.

"I call upon the great Mother, as one of the fruit that hang from Her limbs, to enlighten Her daughters with a vision of Her great and wise plan, so that the rot of fear may find no home in this daughter's heart."

Athena stepped in front of Mercurio, who hunched his shoulders to kneel down further, until his black hair draped over his face and forehead and brushed the carpet.

Muscles worked under his patchwork collection of tattoos, which declared obsessive devotion to Athena and at least two other mistresses. They were intermixed with Catholic and Pagan symbols executed with various degrees of skill.

The cat-of-nine-tails struck the decorated flesh loudly, the wet sound of the multiple tongues making their vicious strike preceded by a keening whistle that Mary Ellen knew by her practised ear proved how uncompromising a blow Mercurio was suffering. He showed no reaction. Athena struck him ten more such blows before pausing to speak.

"Mother, we offer a humble gift, the pain and blood of this man, by nature your prodigal child. He is a blessed martyr, for he has known the sublime echo of being cast in Your likeness, and found himself unworthy of the demands. For his bravery and righteousness in renouncing his sisterhood, we honour him and make him Your sacrifice."

Then Athena stood, mad eyes squeezed tight, back straight,

breath suspended so that firm white breasts, slatted ribcage appeared sculpted from ivory. The cat drooped in her fist, gaudy tongues brushing the floor. The music had broken through to a plateau of less intensity and was now percolating along with bass synthesiser and tabla.

Marina, who obviously knew her cues, walked on her knees to the sideboard and fetched a silver serving tray, soldiering back in the same manner so as to proffer the burden up to her stony-eyed goddess.

The tray was arranged with a small, squat jar cut from amber, a surgical scalpel with a large scallop of a blade fit into a heavy black handle, and a napkin made of rough-woven linen.

At Athena's nod Marina set the tray down before her mistress's bare feet. The black-clad transsexual carefully unscrewed the brass lid from the jar and held it so Athena could crook one long, pale middle finger inside.

The finger came out caked with a black paste. She bent down and thickly traced Marina's mouth with it, on top of the dark crimson lipstick already there. Sweat broke forth immediately on Marina's wrinkled forehead. *A scalding unguent or some primitive drug?* Mary Ellen debated.

Athena dipped the same finger into the jar once more, and now turned to Mercurio. His legs were folded under him, eyes cast down, patiently awaiting the second stage of his sacrifice.

His mistress lifted his head by his unshaven jaw, and penetrated his mouth with her stiff finger, fucking it like a cunt while she rubbed the paste around inside.

"Touch the floor with the back of your head," she instructed him.

Without rising from his knees, Mercurio immediately bent his spine backwards until he was pulled into the shape of a tightly drawn bow. The candlelight reflected the faint spray of freckles in an intimate place as Athena lifted a long leg and straddled her slave above his popping eyes, facing his thighs.

Abruptly, she squatted, flexing her hard flanks, driving her ass hard into Mercurio's face. The part of Mary Ellen that couldn't help but enjoy such kinky ceremony was stirred, even though she was becoming more and more impatient and disappointed; Athena's crypto-mystical sex and drug games weren't going to teach her more about the Black.

She was stuck here, though, and felt stupid. How did you politely excuse yourself during a moment like this? You don't. After several grinding revolutions of her slim hips, Athena gestured to Marina, and her other servant brought the tray near.

Athena grasped the scalpel handle with both hands, drawing it for practice several times against Mercurio's colourfully inked chest, as if she were a samurai practising to help another commit *seppuku*. Things seemed about to get messy.

Mary Ellen held her breath, thinking of how crazed Athena sometimes seemed when she was in scenes at the clubs.

The cut was insistently long and lavishly deep, running the full length of Mercurio's quivering sternum. He shuddered violently but strained forward to receive the blade's painful kiss. The dark cascade began to well forth from the gash in his belly before the slice was even completed.

Athena brought the scalpel up before her lips in a formal gesture. Then, with the self-conscious wickedness of a little girl, she stuck out a shockingly pink triangular tongue to gingerly steal a few drops of blood from the sticky, razored edge.

Carefully sucking the blade clean, she then let some of the blood drool off her lips as her head lolled back, that long red hair now dangling against the small of her well-exercised ass.

Then, after a wracking shudder of her own, Athena released a rowdy stream of piss that splattered all over Mercurio's face, exploding in a noisy spray like a waterfall crashing against jagged rock. Mary Ellen could hear some of it strike hollowly against the back of Mercurio's open throat.

Now a wicked black foam came fizzing and rising from the loose juncture where Athena's cunt met Mercurio's mouth; streaming across the slave's face and chest, sizzling where it funnelled into the fresh wound. Her copious piss had acted as some sort of catalyst to the paste, and suddenly the drawing room stunk from the clash of some sharp spice with an equally exotic flowery scent.

"*Your horse is saddled, Mother! Ride this low beast and use it as You would, only grant us Your presence,*" Athena declared, gazing out the open window towards the moon.

Daintily, she swung one pale leg to the side and dismounted the bloody slave, who remained arched and motionless.

In the next moment the flesh on Mary Ellen's arms prickled beneath their leather gauntlets, and she felt a cold wave break in the pit of her belly.

With a violent howl, Mercurio leapt straight up into the air in an impossible arc, a casual flip that sent a thin rain of blood spraying away from him. Two drops kissed Athena's cheek; one burst on the back of Mary Ellen's knuckle.

Marina cowered at her mistress's knee as Athena's other slave landed deftly on his hands and feet, crouched into a lupine pose. Mercurio, dripping blood from his still open wound onto the hardwood floor, still foaming at the mouth, growled. His eyes were rolled back to the whites, but Mary Ellen somehow had the feeling those blind eggs were boring straight into her.

She was startled when he spoke in a voice that was not his hormone-assisted male parody, but a sexless, sly whisper, barbed with barely hidden teeth.

"Little sister! Little human sister, I see that you can see! The talk of you is true! The never-ending has kissed a mortal's eyes!"

Mary Ellen hadn't noticed before how long Mercurio's ears

were, which now lay back, or how pointed his nose, which now twitched with the scent of her, obvious to him even from under her leather and vinyl. No longer spastic and tense, the muscles were now working under the colourful skin of his back in sinuous self-pleasure, primal and confident. He spoke again.

"Little Sister, do not fear me. I am old to you, but a young god, as gods on this plane go. I have known and strode this land since before the days of the first of your kind, those dark, simple ones who respected me well and provided the food of their love.

"Now there are the millions of you, pale and crafty and self-obsessed, or dark, bitter and corrupted by misery. The confusion and hate you have for yourselves grieves me, so I stay in my world, in the mountains beyond the clouds. I visit only when a clean soul calls, and even then only when it amuses me. But you, Little Sister, I could not miss the chance to meet you, to see you with this horse's eyes."

Mary Ellen was mesmerised, barely aware of Athena staring in incomprehension at the creature that so recently been her hermaphroditic slave.

"Do not despair, Little Sister, though your gift is a great stone to bear, and will doubtless consume much of your earthly life, and remove you from the pleasures you once knew. But take heart, sister. You are now but a step away from the Dreaming, and someday we will make love in my lands, when you have completed your service to the Never-Ending. We shall howl together in a song more beautiful than you have ever known."

The still-crouched Mercurio stuck his ass higher in the air, and waved it provocatively. Mary Ellen found the nerve to speak.

"Who is the Never-Ending" she asked, airless lungs turning her voice thin. Mercurio barked and grinned, his eyes still blank.

"You have prayed to the Never-Ending, Little Sister, or at least to the dimmest reflection of its smallest mote. You have kissed the cross, have you not? You were taught to by your father and mother, who were too lost in simple human ritual to feel the real touch of Its endless fingers. It knows you, as a mother knows her children, and all your family, too, and watches even as they strive to come home.

"I am as much Its child as you; I am merely more wise and powerful, and longer-lived. I have seen others like you, and watched as they folded in on themselves in grief at the burden of their gifts. Do not despair, sister. Put aside the aimless dream of the life you have known, and let service to the other worlds free your soul. Bask in your forbidden knowledge."

Finished with advice, Mercurio howled and leaped upon his mistress, who had stood all this time by a lush Victorian sofa, watching proudly as her slave was possessed by a powerful god called down through her own supplications.

Athena didn't recoil or call out at the attack; instead, she fell back on the divan, legs splayed open. Ready to receive the Coyote between them. Her own eyes now rolled back.

Evidencing an impossible strength, the short-statured Mercurio lifted his mistress as if she were a doll, and set her on all fours. Her head fell forward, hair a crimson waterfall against the carpet, nipples crushed against her breasts by her slave's fingers, which curled like talons and pressed so deeply they summoned blood.

Mercurio hunched over her back, eyes rimmed red, ears now even longer, and laid back flat against his smooth hair. His teeth gnashed together, spittle flying as he ground them and beat his limp flap of skin between the split in Athena's haunches.

Mary Ellen quietly rose from her seat and edged toward the door, snatching her long black coat as she went. Marina stared at her accusingly, as if she had brought a more virulent degree of madness into the household than usual. The transvestite was also doubtless unhappy not be included in the proceedings.

Still, she was a faithful if dour servant. Mary Ellen turned the front door knob as gently as possible, watching as Marina fetched a solid crystal rod, about eight inches long, from the sideboard and headed purposefully toward the rutting couple.

Tiny grunts leaked from within the curtain of hair covering Athena's face, and a clear fluid fell from between her legs in one long, lazy runnel and caught the candlelight.

Mary Ellen let herself out.

She stayed with her back to the front door of the building until she saw an open cab cruising slowly enough down the street to be hailed from the stoop.

Though the car's interior stunk of some sickly-sweet incense, she kept the windows rolled up all the way to her apartment, slumping down against the bench so that nothing out there in the Black could catch her eye.

When she returned to her apartment even the splay of mail inside the battered box in her apartment building lobby seemed portentous. She left it untouched, mounting the sloping stairs as swiftly as she could.

A warm bath eventually slowed the jackhammer beating of her heart, though she once imagined creaks outside the bolted bathroom door, and the scraping of four sets of claws against the splintered wood of her apartment's floorboards.

XV

Homicide Detective Mickey O'Farrell was *goddamn* hungry. His thickly-carpeted slab of belly ached intermittently, contracting around its empty core so spastically he occasionally fell into a brief, wracking shiver. Here came one now, making him wrap his overcoat more tightly around his oversized torso.

His trench coat was a badly-made, exorbitantly overpriced 56 long from one of the big and tall men's stores on Lower Broadway. Twenty bucks knocked off, though, when he had flashed his badge. Big deal; he still had to be careful not to flex his shoulders too much or pull the seams loose.

He wondered if the slow-moving, grinding elevator that now shook under his size-fifteen feet would truly support his bulk all the way up to the fifth floor of this fleabag. The Livonia was one of the most criminally maintained transient hotels he'd ever set massive foot in.

He pictured the cables snapping and him ending up in the

basement, brushing off his torn, ruined clothes and swiftly limping off lest his survival be regarded as a miracle by some cocaine-addled janitor hiding from his shift boss.

How depressing. Here he was visiting another animal hospital, yet another dangerously unsound holding pen for the sick and defective members of the herd. But then that was his job.

Broken elevators? There were much more frequent pitfalls and senseless complications to dwelling in this, the most famous city of his livestock's proud yet decadent modern age.

Living Overground had been a tough adjustment in the first place; he would have been perfectly content living as his ancestors did, in the great buried caverns far to the North and halfway around the globe.

There, you were lost down deep enough to be sheltered from the direct wrath of the countless tons of ice and snow, and the petulant ire of old One-eyed Wotan, the all-powerful warrior and meddling uncle whose spectre was used to keep the youngest ogres frightened into manageability.

But fate's river inexorably flowed, and truth be told, the enforced solitude O'Farrell sometimes felt he was drowning in here in this city did boast a positive side.

For instance, his third cousin Jorn Fafwuld's blood oath was still binding, if Fafwuld indeed survived somewhere on this extravagantly huge globe.

The oath had been sworn against O'Farrell when, in a moment of brutish passion, the latter had cracked the spine of Jorn's human wife while raping her for sport one brisk winter solstice eve, while her husband was out breaking the neck of a ram so she could roast it for dinner.

O'Farrell had been embarrassed and penitent after his crime. The bluff, mightily scarred Fafwuld had suffered a certain notoriety for his wilful rebellion against the common-sense laws of both ogre and nature when he had ring-bonded with the prissy and fragile, sharply yammering human female he had stolen during a raid on a modest human encampment whose citizens had fed the entire clan for a full week.

But despite his askew taste in mates, Fafwuld remained an admirable soul, one who would generously invite his cousins along for the harvesting of a weakened, hallucinating human hunting party that was easily slaughtered while struggling through the snow in their vain campaign for stag or bear. Before he had even plucked up the prime choice cuts himself, he would let his most ardent soldiers choose.

Recalling one such hunt, O'Farrell wistfully thought those simple days to be the finest of his life. He often imagined that if his crudely hewn, gigantic race had been gifted with the ephemeral power to whirl and play inside their unconscious heads that the humans casually called dream and so maddeningly took for granted, he would by force of despairing will return whenever his eyes closed to the comfortingly blank expense of ice and snow that in the predawn starlight of some hunts would stretch enticingly to every horizon, bathed in the great uninterrupted intangibility of misted earth and sky.

On a fine day such as that, O'Farrell would listen to his beard hairs crackle in the sub-zero wind, and ardently suck the clean new moisture from the instantly forming frost encrusting his bare lips. He and his brothers and cousins would lie in wait for the succulent meals that inevitably blundered on a straight line right into the always-hungry ogre clan's hard, huge bellies. They would emerge grinning from their caverns to confront their prey, the polished joints of bear thighs dangling confidentially from cloth-wrapped fingers, ready to tame any futile instinct towards fight or flight.

During the subsequent harvest, the blood would crystallise into a ruby blanket upon the hoarfrost, and the steam from the opened bodies would melt the icicles in O'Farrell's eyebrows.

Yes, though unbearably cold to many of its human dwellers, New York City in late January was no good place for an ogre. With his thick blood and gristly, towering build he found it nearly balmy. August was unspeakable; every year O'Farrell would cope by robbing some of his victims and, all the while uncomfortable that he might attract attention, pay for the Waldorf's most lavish suite.

He'd run the monstrous air conditioner on high and order up an unceasing bucket brigade of ice from incredulous but unquestioning room service, dumping them over his belly, cursing to himself at the way his ass was uncomfortably wedged into the insufficient dimensions of the suite's supposedly luxurious blue marble and porcelain tub.

His appetite even lessened during the punishing summers here.

But New York City was the ground where, in his wilful ignorance, he had chosen to make his stand, as one of what was probably the final generation of his kind. During the last hundred years, the vague tales of the metropolis's urban valleys and canyons full of shadows and easy meals had filtered to the caverns, and his goal had been set.

As he had discovered, the food truly was plentiful and easily secured. And as well, here in the great melting pot of freakish humanity that crowded worse than the flies around the great garbage ditch by the commons, he could blend in here like nowhere else that he had seen on his arduous journey across this too-large land called America.

By the time he got to New York City, he had learned about identification papers. Once he paid someone to forge them, a real job was easy. The police academy recruitment officer, a fat white human with a crew cut, had wet his lips when O'Farrell manoeuvred his juggernaut build in through the office door.

"This'll show those we-bes. A good Aryan boy like you will

kick those niggers' asses! Bring some respect back to the force, like in LA."

O'Farrell had no idea what the man was hissing about, but learned shortly thereafter, when he had gone apartment hunting in the wrong section of Brooklyn. He was lucky not to have been shot; the three black youths who had tried to mug him ended up as unsolved homicides instead.

He suspected certain instructors of like sympathies to his recruitment officer were regularly massaging his written test grades so that the racially pure giant was kept a few rungs safely up from failure. His sort was needed on the street.

Yes, he had to admit, America was the land of opportunity.

Which was why, he supposed, so many other foreign-born Feeders seemed to immigrate here. Sometimes O'Farrell couldn't turn his great bulk around on an overcrowded subway car without bumping into the displaced or migrated scion of yet another ancient race, often as not decadent and full of lassitude with city living's easy availability of food.

Some of the most primitive species were not only disgusting but troublesome. Only yesterday, he had just missed a nip on his huge, stubby index finger perfumed by ogre shit and human viscera, when he'd been bushwhacked by an Amphisbaena that had set up roost in the pungent darkness of the unscrubbed garbage cans piled behind the solitary giant's tar-roofed shack nestled under the Brooklyn Bridge.

The shack was his hidden den. He never allowed any of his fellow officers or partners to drop him off, for fear the flayed and carved flesh that hung curing in the clay-floored room in the back might demand their attention with its ripe aromas.

O'Farrell suspected himself paranoid; the five human senses were all so profoundly dull that Feeders of the most grotesquely alien or jarringly odd stripe could somehow achieve proper camouflage in the millions of shadows holding together the bones of this ugly, endless city, a mad and waste-ful world unto itself that packed more living creatures and their garbage into a smaller space than the cavern-keeps of the most modestly peopled clan of his ancient, sluggish race.

Like the Amphisbaena. He hadn't even the time to be dis-mayed at his reacquaintance with the filth-sucking serpent that had been an occasional and gross nuisance in the darker, damper crevices of his clan's keep, manifesting themselves mostly in the vicinity of those cracks that his grandfather informed him led directly to the earth's molten core.

The twin heads of the bad-tempered vermin darted in a quick, spastic feint at O'Farrell's ponderously oversized hand. If the scrappy beast's congenital nearsightedness hadn't led it to misjudge the arc of attack, two sets of fangs would have broken O'Farrell's flesh, both slobbering their shares of wrenchingly swift paralytic into his blood.

Instead the stuff sprayed ineffectually against the dirt, mak-ing a candy bar wrapper bubble and fold in on itself. The venom was as black and greasy as the shiny stones the ogre had sometimes found half-buried in the walls of certain cav-erns back home. It would turn a human's flesh dark as a blood blister and bloat it to twice its elasticity in seconds, burning out the victim's nervous system with the same violence of hunger as the grease fires that burst forth without herald and kissed the cavern's ceiling when Gunder Quarterson, the self-appointed clan gourmet, would unseal a too-tightly stoppered cooking pot.

O'Farrell remained motionless, confronting this cousin of the nasty little scavengers from the Old World, where the flab-by, scaly folds of flesh hot to the touch would improbably sprout mangy collars of ivory-hued wool to cushion their flat, ungraceful skulls. Here in this warmer clime, there was no such decoration.

Without warning, the giant had stamped down on the thing, fairly confident of the protection afforded by the great leather boots that he concealed beneath enormously baggy trousers. The boots had been custom-made by an incredulous Brooklyn cobbler to the size and thickness of the pair O'Farrell's father had gifted his son with on the proud occasion of his first killing day.

Predictably, each head chose to attack the closest side of his calf. He reached down and grabbed them right under each jaw and triumphantly plucked the hissing monster from the garbage-strewn dirt. The brother heads sought each other's company; outflanked, it was trying to return to flight mode, where it would clutch one head with the other's mouth and writhe away in loopy but disconcertingly swift cartwheels.

Wearily, O'Farrell caught up each extravagantly whiskered dragon's head between huge thumb and forefinger. Sighing and turning his head away, he squeezed as hard as he could, holding the thrashing corpse out away from his body so the poison wouldn't splatter his fingers or his already distressed trench coat.

Not a single part of this useless little creature was edible; he threw it away in an empty ashcan, stuffing a layer of mouldy newspaper over it that he lit with a disposable lighter. At least the things burned swiftly to ash.

Such was life in his ugly shack. Inside, he had made a vain attempt to evoke the grand, glittering ice caves of the Northland. The scattered, poorly cured throwskins of what had been his more visually attractive meals, along with a couple of impatient, abandoned attempts at recreating the bone altars the clan's shaman would construct and keep in perpetual repair, succeeded only in inadvertent parody.

Being second cousin to the Frost Giants, O'Farrell was not famous among his kind for being exceedingly tasteful or crafty. But he was self-aware enough to recognise the depressing futility of his feeble efforts at keeping his culture alive.

Thus the disconsolate, flesh-eating giant wallowed in self-mockery and a voluntary state of near total discomfort. Only during the most freezing days of the winter did he feel the vitality a strapping, well-fed ogre who had not yet even reached middle-age should know.

It was only on those days when a respectable storm froze the city to a standstill, did O'Farrell look at the sky and smile to himself, briefly rescued from the inevitable violent secretions of profuse amounts of his particularly rowdy scent, a luxuriously fatty odour fed by the overstuffed humans he consumed to forget his homesickness.

But still and again, like the spells the shaman would sometimes gift the clan with, he clung to his refrain: The hunting was trouble-free, and the menu's diversity unimpeachable. Tender babies, supple young women; ripe, smooth young boys, and, truth be told, even the occasional grizzled old wino or chicken-limbed whore.

Too often, he was woken from his unpleasantly light slumbers seized by a sudden urge to commit lip-smacking mayhem, ears ringing with the growls of his not easily-satisfied belly. Clamouring for its owner's attention, O'Farrell's generous stomach demanded meat even when the rest of him was dizzy with weariness. Or, as occurred with increasing frequency the last year or so, numbed into clumsiness by the compulsive consumption of obscenely massive amounts of the watery, tasteless mead so poorly brewed by his inept prey, spiced with the slightly more tart and pleasant tickle of sour mash whiskey.

No matter what his state, at such moments his only choice was to squeeze behind the wheel of his '71 Lincoln Continental and go hunting. Though you couldn't tell from the outside, the bench seat had been ripped free and pushed as far as it would go against the rear seat; his weight kept it steady underneath him as he would steer the car's long, crumpled fenders all the way to the Lincoln Tunnel corridor, where a small but dependable stock of the least chewy, most juicy street meat constantly grazed for crumpled twenties and drugs.

The elevator arrived at the fifth floor. He pulled back the manual doors, revealing that the cab had admitted defeat three inches below floor level. He squeezed up through the space, and wondered how quickly he could do what he had to here and make a much-needed detour right now over to the Lincoln Tunnel.

By the most casual irony, it was his own fault that he was working overtime, an hour into Homicide's midnight shift. He would much rather have been at home, sprawled in the ripening nurture of the gory, claustrophobic shack that was for all its failings indeed his home. He wanted to be masturbating into the scooped-clean skull of the Asian masseuse whose jawbone he had gnawed down to the white in merely a half hour only two nights ago, though the satisfaction of that meal was already old and dim.

Instead of eating, O'Farrell was stuck investigating one of his own victims. Not entirely a rare occurrence, but usually his meals were classified missing persons with strong suspicion of foul play. In such cases, O'Farrell framed a couple of humans for some meals, just to keep his case record looking good.

This time though, he had left the corpse behind. It had not been a hunt. He did not desire its meat, and felt safe that there was no way the crime could be connected to him.

It had been a mercy killing, an alien act he had never been provoked to commit even in the unforgiving ecology of the frozen Motherland.

The late Miranda Angela Davis, aka Taiwantha Rodgers aka

Bunnyhole had been a crack whore by trade. Absolutely unappetizing to him in any way, alive or put to sleep; he turned queasy at food so rickety and juiceless. Even if you forced it down — ignoring the sickly aftertastes and thin corpuscle gruel — by a few hours later, you'd be left with nothing but a unsated appetite and a red plastic bucket half-full of sucked-clean joints and never more than a baker's dozen of teeth, crunchy nuggets which although not uncrackable to his own diamond-hard molars, were always spoiled bitter by cavities. They brought the most amusement, being spit from across the room into the bucket, daring bank shots skipping across the sticky rim. Marrow aftertaste? Not enough to speak of.

There was also a matter of clan honour to uphold, even in this madhouse world. He considered himself a noble hunter, and would not feed on sick or lame beasts. Although the humans were his food, he didn't enjoy seeing any but the most unlikeable of them suffer for longer than the one long, horrid moment of realisation that their time was really up that wrote itself across their faces at the moments of their deaths. He was intimate with this final, frozen expression, on his victims and on his hapless professional clients, as well.

It was the curse of mortality, and his race suffered from their own strain of it; they were after all made from the same dust as the animals they fed upon. Giants were not shades, demons, djinn, or Valkyrie; nor demi-gods moving sideways through the unseen world, popping up for unexpected appearances ranging in consequence from merely distracting to body and soul-threatening.

They were also less mystical than the shapeshifters, or the walking dead; all the intertwined races of vampire and zombie and were-creature, from the tengu and the lamia to the coyote and the walking wolves. Though O'Farrell had in fact lunched on a walking wolf at a certain juncture, met in Central Park one winter's eve. Once past the gamy stink, he found himself immersed in a superbly satisfying meal.

Certainly by human ken the giants and ogres seemed immortal, their races were so long-lived. But the unavoidable spectre that equally haunted O'Farrell's kind from birth inspired some sympathy for the most common, youngest race.

In the same way, O'Farrell's understanding of the quality of mercy was indeed rather strained, by the morals of the people he lived among. For instance — though the urbanised but still hardly sophisticated brute was a rapist by species, his brutal assaults on human women — and the occasional long-haired, feminine young man — smacked less of sadism, or the need to bolster a petty human male ego, than the most extravagantly thoughtless selfishness.

O'Farrell agonised or gloried no more tearing open his meal first with his cock and rubbing the engorged head against its pulsing liver just before he ate to relieve an uncomfortably heavy erection than did the mortal shepherd who unemotionally relieved himself into the warm, tight accommodation of a lamb before preparing it for his family's dining board.

So the ogre felt no guilt, standing there returned to the scene of his crime. The musty fifth floor of the residence hotel offered a choice of ten peeling doors all so narrow he would have had to turn sideways to squeeze through. The baggy, torn carpeting was matted to a near shag with the same pungence of filth as would line the unkempt cavern nest of an old, sickly father who shat himself in his sleep, knowing the Little Nothing for one last time before the farewell party held for him by his children, as his neck was cracked by his most beloved offspring and corpse incinerated in a pyre that lasted three days.

A wild-eyed old lady was peeking at O'Farrell from behind her half-open door: Number 5975. Right next to his victim's room, which was number 5997, a figure O'Farrell idly wondered might not represent the date of Miranda's reincarnation.

He was a simple ogre, free of serious spiritual inclination beyond a childish affection for the brazenly adversarial, good-humoured exploits of the Thunder God, as well as the occasional shiver summoned to greet a barely surfaced recollection of some cautionary childhood fable. But he was convinced that such signs regularly occurred. One only had to look for them with open eyes, as both the shaman and his grandfather had told him.

The ratty blue hair barely covered the nosy hall monitor's freckled scalp, the old bitch glumly marking O'Farrell's path past her door with the same rapt fear a toreador's second tracks a bull's first lumber across the killing floor.

"NYPD, ma'am," O'Farrell intoned, turning on his heel to face her without warning, and allowing the heavy badge pinned to the leather folder flop down from the obscurity of his huge paw. He had learned the right way to brandish his badge by watching television and practising along; one of the few modern luxuries he allowed himself in his lair, he had tapped into a power line for electricity only so he could have cable; a cave dweller, his eyesight was sharper than his wits.

Watching the Super Station, where a lot of police dramas could be found, he immediately bonded with Cannon, the big fat man who solved crimes while buried in a constant film of sweat, mopping his drenched brow as he huffed and puffed the air into his flab-entombed lungs in between stentorian declarations of the inevitably of the American justice system — the most toothless and morbid, corrupt law O'Farrell had ever encountered, short of the codes governing some of the serpent races.

He imagined that William Conrad, the actor who played Cannon, would make a real feast. Showing an unexpected appreciation of camp, the ogre was delighted by his widely popular portrayal of a character even more ridiculously impossible than those conjured by the tale-spinners for the rapt, youthful audiences he had been a part of.

"They took her away already. She'd lost a sock. I told them to go back for it, but they ignored me. One guy joked to the other, pretending like I wasn't even there, 'she'll never have to worry about her socks matching again.' Is that respect? What did I pay taxes all my life for, to be made fun of by some big-nosed little jungle bunny when I die?

"Poor little thing, though: Her men were the death of her, and every one of them some shade of nigger, from Hershey's syrup to malted milk. She was so sad all the time; she would talk to me about her old boyfriends, always saying she was waiting for some rich guy who made porn movies, but was gonna quit doin' them, for her, and who was going to come back any day from some shady kind of business deal in Hawaii and take her out to Long Island so that she'd never have to leave again."

Disgusted with the vindictive, smug tone in which the sharp-eyed biddy offered such an intimate map of her former neighbour's vulnerability, O'Farrell felt the same oddly resonant twinge of sympathy for the dead whore that had inspired him to grant her death in the first place.

O'Farrell already knew her story too well; he had observed Miranda several times in both his official and more discreet, personally motivated surveillances before deciding it would be proper to aid the always-trembling thing's sodden quest to achieve the fate she sought but which she could not look in the glassy, cooling eye.

Everybody's toilet paper; john, pimp, cop, the other hookers, occasionally vans full of grim-faced and muscular young white men in Izod shirts that everybody else knew to run from as soon as it turned a corner. Once they had left used hypodermics gathered from the gutter jammed through her breasts.

The classic easy mark, she was no hassle to haul in during streetwalker sweeps slow nights, when arrest quotas were not being filled.

She was a perpetual clubfoot, stumbling through the hungry, extravagantly debased and diseased dance of what O'Farrell could only think of as Hole Need conducted every afternoon and evening on the windy sidewalks of the West Side factory district that bordered ten straight blocks below the Lincoln Tunnel, on the banks of the poisoned Hudson River, where the bloated bodies of those who had lost their place in human society would finally rise to the top, engorged skin ready to split and free the evil gases brewing within.

She was not too loud or disruptive on the street, except for the occasional three-day binge when she would wander in circles wailing senseless lyrics of grief about an uncle who had raped her at her mother's funeral. Enough, though, to spook the livelier of the animated corpses that were her competition. Sisters only through profession, they would shake their heads and step sideways down the block, checking their tiny clutches for the fifth time that half hour to count again how few vials left.

Miranda's dissolution and plain features were unremarkable and dreary, not evoking contempt, contemplation or sadistic desire of any kind in her peer group. Impotent and invisible, she was doubly-cursed by being just bright enough to be aware of her state.

O'Farrell was surprised to find her condition a bit too familiar to rest easily in his thoughts, which due to his intellectual heritage would intermittently scramble themselves and start over from close to scratch.

The Feeder homicide detective watched from his unmarked each evening as her pimp, in his ostentatiously business-like way, would strip her of her stem and substitute a long, curled strip of cheapest brand Trojans.

O'Farrell knew her owner wouldn't let her glimpse that treasured sliver of brown-streaked glass until she had turned a minimum of a half-dozen tricks. He would yawn and dig in his lap, scratching his massive, flea-bitten balls as he shook his head at his own sentimentality, watching her collapse her cheeks frantically around one wormy little human cock after another. If she had rebelled at the uncompromising pace with which she received customers, her pimp had soft, reproving syllables ready to murmur in her infected ear before — if she was lucky — settling for a single, theatrically-delivered bitch-slap.

Since hapless Miranda was far too timid and resigned to raise a single protest over working conditions, she escaped such punishment. She had to contend instead with the braintwisties, the unpredictable spasms of addiction which might mercifully numb her out with their deep stabs to her cortex and the back of her throat, or then again might turn around and bring it all into perfect clarity, so she could feel the contemptuous, inefficient yet brutal pumpings of her pussy, her mouth, her asshole, by a parade of perspiring businessmen and snickering homeboys, as well as the real social outcasts, who didn't even have the manners for a cat house, the inevitable slithering unclean murderers who lack not in imagination but courage.

It was disgusting, the depths to which these humans dragged each other down.

O'Farrell had given serious and focused thought to just tearing the goddamn pimp limb from limb instead, no fuss, a lot of muss. Too easy to fall prey to irritation inspired by the jittery, thin little man with the tree-coloured flesh and razor-creased cheek. But why bother? That permanently damaged, self-hating beast who didn't even feel the gravel that stuck to her knees would only find another version of him, another convenient path to her passive suicide.

Besides, an ogre rarely kills what he doesn't intend to eat, and though his appetite was great, O'Farrell never gorged himself until forced to vomit, as ogre children so often did after feasting on the four-legged subjugates of man, the dogs and horses and pigs stolen from the farms; a collection of species not graced with such possessive guardianship as the humans, which could be consumed at whim.

He still remembered absorbing the Feeding rules when he was an infant. Nearly five hundred years ago, endless, whispered rote assailed him as he nestled cool and full in his crib, unaware he was enjoying the last days of the great ice caverns.

A golden era it was, before humanity's ever-threatening technology forced his extended family's furtive, hurried abandonment of their ancestral home. Though not what it once was, the clan was still strong, and could have easily mowed down several armies. There were those bold enough to suggest their efforts may have even led to a triumphantly grisly campaign to harvest the arrogant prey, and colonise their empty nests. Such an action might have been the first step in the righteous reclamation of earth's dominion from the stupid and the weak.

But every ogre of the clan had been indoctrinated to accept on faith what the awful response would be to such an overt act of hostility. By the soldier-assassins who were to the giants what the giants were to humanity. Feed too indiscriminately on the human meat, and they would attract the vengeance of the dominions, the archangels — perhaps even, if a Feeder victory supplied a pile of atrocities high enough, the rare notice of the hated seraphs themselves.

In their rough hearts, all of the clan knew an ill-considered invasion of a human city would be the same as suicide. The end result would have been the devastation of their own people, instead, and O'Farrell knew it as surely as he knew it was his duty to put an ailing beast out of its misery, no matter how insignificant the creature's station.

This suspicious old woman was a perfect example. By her sheer ugliness, O'Farrell would not have disputed her if she had laid claim to having suckled at a Norn queen's breast. The hag tried to peer into the hallway to see his great hands fumble as he fitted the night clerk's passkey in her late neighbour's door.

The inhuman homicide detective was tickled by how the old biddy was afraid to creep out another lousy inch from behind the ineffectual shelter of a door already splintered around the lock from some previous burglary. He could have walked over and shoved his open hand through it with hardly any effort, and knocked her back into her closet.

"She had a baby, she would talk about it, going to get it but she didn't know where it was, said the government took it away from her, but I'll bet that's only half the story," the crone warily confided.

A clumsy attempt to exchange secrets with this hulking, beetle-browed stranger in the ill-fitting suit and trench coat, who wasn't offering her any refreshing draughts of someone else's pain and degradation. Her tone tended to waver between poles of sympathy and disapproval, unpleasantly prickly with fraudulent concern at either extreme.

"Several children, as far we know, ma'am," he told the woman.

"We found the liver of one of them fried up on the deceased's hot plate so expertly, we suspect she may have had an alias as a short-order cook," he concluded, shading his delivery with a grim, conversation-stopping grumble so ridiculously like Frank Cannon's he had to strive mightily to keep his gaze flinty, and not break down in a fit of mirth.

In his hunger, he was conjuring the sight of that slim,

shaven Filipino whore's liver, which was indeed soaking in a pot of vinegar back at his shack, waiting not to be fried but simply boiled into what O'Farrell considered a gourmet meal. Ah, another decadence: cooked meat, in the Old Country, had been frowned upon, a sign of the ogre race's degeneration and growing weakness.

That was another situation which constantly haunted him. He still remembered the scrapes along the ceiling of the huge cavern that had served as clan commons, the brittle, elegant stalactites snapped clean off in unpredictable direction where his great grandfather always managed to bump his knot-ridden head.

When O'Farrell reached his full growth, it dawned on the mortified youth he would have needed to be half again as large to brush the longest stalactite's tip with his straining fingertips.

But the killing blow against the clan was struck through the unprecedented onslaught of the human presence. Weak little babies once, they had bred for five thousand years as frantically as insects; finally their sheer numbers were enough to dampen the clan's stubborn spirit.

Hunting quietly was harder and harder, now that the humans seemed to always arrive in well-choreographed groups, and loaded with telecommunications equipment, so that the most bushwhacked explorers would have had a chance to betray the clan's existence to the rest of their honourless race before dying.

After a few near disasters during small-scale forays into the most removed of the outlying villages, the clans folk were stunned to hear their leader Olaf Grey Eye announce he was ready to embrace the greater wisdom of retreat.

Only four days later, the entire clan had fragmented to the four corners of the planet, sent to make refuge in whatever sympathetic regions they could discover.

And on that day O'Farrell heard his adult given name for the last time. He had never liked it much anyway. Augeur Horrfblaast he had been dubbed, in satire of a monumentally uncomfortable and embarrassingly loud adolescent bout with flatulence inspired by a whelp's rash meal of snow leopard soaked in man's poisons.

Marching out into the Great White Nothing with his meagre share of the clan's gold and jewels, draped in three of his favourite human skins, the barely mature Horrfblaast immediately fell out of contact with the others, stubbornly marching into the heart of a lightning storm. The skins had been singed off his reddened back; the gold melted against his flesh. Working it free had been unpleasant.

Even after he learned through trial and error how to blend-in reasonably well with the herd, making it all the way down to North America strained the young ogre's wits and resources to the limit, since he didn't yet trust the bizarre human methods of "rapid transit."

Though strong and thick-headed, the soon-to-be O'Farrell belonged after all to a basically sedentary race possessed by a powerful burrowing instinct.

He gave himself over to this biological destiny when he reached New York City, and stood gripped by wonder, buried sweetly in the profound shadows under the Brooklyn Bridge. Like so many before him, he became by choice a citizen of New York City.

Now nothing could draw him away from the five boroughs, not even the yearning in his groin for the use of his rutting mate and possible breeding bitch as well. The lissom Ruddhilda MacLir was a bewitchingly spare 300-pound pouting beauty with sleek thighs no thicker than baby tree trunks for whom he had religiously saved the testicles from any successfully stalked mountain climbers or archaeologists who came searching the clan's homeland for proof of their own puny tribe's mewling birth throes.

There was never any such proof hidden in our mountains, anyway, or we would have seen it, O'Farrell thought bitterly in the middle of his perfunctory search of Miranda's small room, finally out of sight of the prying old biddy next door.

He sought provocative but ultimately meaningless trinkets he could neatly tag and bag to prove to his squad lieutenant he was doing his job. A cryptic note that would send his colleagues chasing ghosts would have been nice, but his reading and writing were still barely at sixth grade level, and he felt the deception beyond him. He had felt secure in his identity, however when he learned over a third of the other police were no better educated.

He carelessly lifted the iron-framed bed with one hand, and found a crushed bouquet of desiccated roses, wrapped in the sort of cheap paper the all-night delis used. He tried to pick up a brown to and drop it into the evidence bag, but as his huge fingers brushed its surface, the fragile interlocking spirals of ruined petals rattled and then disintegrated into a fine brown ash.

Fucking ignorant humans, O'Farrell thought, his increasingly black mood now coalescing with the fresh bubbling acids in his empty, complaining belly.

They came to drive us from our beautiful, dark home and juice-stained hearth seeking the ghost of a corrupt culture. Now we've been absorbed by them, devoured by our own food, left no proof of our proud, simple heritage except the subtle increase here and there in the human fatality rate around the world. And grudging recognition from the other greater races.

Recognition which, O'Farrell had found, was hardly worth much. He found no more brotherhood with the fellow Feeder races than he did with the humans. He had suffered the chilly, condescending repulsion of more than one vampire; those haughty immortal leeches, intellectual masturbators, secretly fragile bullies that even though not fully of the natural world wouldn't have survived a minute alone on the hoarfrost. He had also felt the xenophobic distrust of the diverse serpent races raised in both arid clime and swampland: the Lamia, the Naga, and so forth.

The giant was particularly irked by the sullen disinterest of the self-possessed incubi and all of the other nightmares.

Every rule demands an exception, however and O'Farrell's most exciting discovery in years had been of a singular and rare hybrid, a black flower that bore the most deadly-sweet perfume. There was one Feeder who was more than snitch or hunting dog to him: there was one that he worshipped, with an obsessive streak that unnerved him.

A voracious and implacable succubus who was the freakish issue of Lamia and vampire, O'Farrell's demon mistress was a deadly and unpredictable package that over the last seven hundred years — she was two centuries O'Farrell's senior — had, among other adventures, enjoyed the worship of a human suicide cult numbering nearly a thousand.

On a Sunday morning of the season, the chosen among the ranks of believers had been charged to cheerfully cut their own throats over massive urns which were then offered up to their laughing deity, who strode into the village under cover of night to frolic and bathe in the stuff, wracked with uncontrollably girlish giggles.

The cult had largely exterminated itself in fifteenth-century Japan, but O'Farrell suspected there were rouge acolytes still to be found, if you wanted to look hard enough. In fact, if he had shared the same innocent awe over his mistress's supernature, he might have been open to offering such a personal tribute.

Not that it would have been demanded. Her tolerance for O'Farrell seemed to border on affection; he amused her, and it was handy to have a brute like him for an occasional accomplice. They had hunted together, a few times. They made a woefully mismatched pair, to blind human eyes. She, so diminutive and of crafty aspect, full of sidelong glances and subtle pursing of the lip; him lumbering and huge, not overly clever.

More often they directed human victims towards one another, politely taking turns picking up the check. She was a rogue princess, and unlike the purer breeds of Feeder nobility, not full of herself, and so did not look down on the cravings of his rough palate, or condemn his ravenous physical appetites as crass.

Sometimes he found himself thinking he would have liked to fuck her, to be able to pound his thick, knobby prick into the human-proportioned slit that he could often smell the briny, acidic secretions from even through her quirky, ornate human fashions. But she would never allow it.

He thought it strange, how lush and hypnotic the promise of her sex was, when in point of fact she was a barren creature from birth, her womb easily imagined as a twisted, sere maze thanks to her rare, precarious marriage of heredities.

As impressions of his demon lover washed over his thoughts, O'Farrell presently remembered with a start another of his pressing worries. Sometimes he pondered if his race's modest mental capacity was its most potent enemy.

He had to go see her, his mistress. Had to seek her out for advice over the unknown human bearing the secret of iron who lurked somewhere out in the city, perhaps the shadowy vanguard of what could be the final extinction of his barely existent race.

Still idly pawing evidence, his roaming attention span was now attracted by this problem: There was something profoundly disturbing about what seemed to his sluggish temporal sense the appearance of this faceless assassin a mere fifty years after the clan had been dispersed.

In the dissolving, uncertain memories of their lore that was taught him as child, there was one commandment above all, the only one not open to interpretation or debate by the shaman and the wise men.

If his kind transgressed too deeply into the house gifted to the most spoiled and beloved race by the seemingly infinite array of gods and their supernatural servants, the unseen maker of this and all worlds would raise a defender of the cattle, a deadly nemesis to any clan that had hunted too boldly out of its keep.

The few Feeders that he had interviewed in passing were aware of the prediction as well. Their versions were sometimes backwards, upsides or even mirror images of the fireside warnings that had made him tremble as a child.

But his sly, inquisitive conspirator would know if there was some connection to be made between the evident murder of the old dragon by a human and this troubling legend. Her unrelenting crafts of seduction would serve as a divining rod to that black pool of extinction-fear standing brackish and silent in his head.

In a leap of logic that made him the ogre equivalent of Albert Einstein, it occurred to O'Farrell that pool must be rippling not only in the back of his simple head, but in the skulls of a great number of the older, wiser and more powerful races, as well.

His was not the only people to degenerate. They had all been systematically reduced by the birth and ascendance of the humans to nomads and refuse, the laughed-at stuff of myth and legend, the harmless cartoons of folklore, now digitised for highest resolution and wired for Dolby.

There were also the rumours of Feeder mass murders, committed by creatures such as those that had peopled his mother's fireside tales of divine avengers sent by the All-Father.

Ridiculous! No street-walking succubus or ghetto werewolf who had told such stories had actually ever seen such apparitions.

They described them, though, the same enormous, inscrutable beings as in the folk tales. Constructed of black fire, gleaming chains, various intricate metals, even sometimes evidencing a finer grade skin than that granted to the silky-fleshed humans.

The superstitious insisted these great avengers hunted with no weapon but a burning light, searing to ash those who transgressed too far against their wilful pets, that craven, spoiled race of Men.

Legend and myth. Perhaps such creatures had once walked the earth, in those far-ago wilder times when various divine creatures strode the planet. But now? The humans' technology had the planet in a death grip, and the Feeders with it.

But his mistress would know the proper course of action. She would help him discover the truth.

He sat on the bed and started rubbing his cock, to distract him from the aching of his belly. Thought more of his mistress. Imagined gleefully what information could be bought and sold with the drug of his malignant voluptuary's singular love, a less immediate but no more merciful venom than that sprayed by the Amphisbaena.

He vaguely understood, having had it explained by her several times, how proximity to her malignant passions encouraged the infection of the human nervous systems with a pernicious toxin she shed that could only be neutralised by the properties present in her chemically unique bodily wastes. As potent and intractable as the saliva drooled by the odd nomadic snow vampire into the new wounds of hapless and doomed ogre and human alike. She was the disease and the cure.

He knew that enslaved humans from all strata of their perversely complex and unfriendly society flocked to grovel before this goddess they mistakenly believe of their kind, ecstatically galvanised by their anguished addiction, wilfully unaware of their role as the drugged and stunned pets of a mistress who could barely be bothered to muster contempt for their twitching bodies, and saw the entire species only as a source of food and as a theatre for the sort of experiments she found entertaining. In fact, sometimes witnessing those pleasures made a mere flesh-eater like him turn queasy at how unclean her process of consumption was.

But that scheming, curious nature could be turned to his advantage: There would be a methodology on locating whatever murderous human was lurking out there... cold iron blade in hand, eager to massacre O'Farrell and all the branches of his many distant, often feuding cousins. Consigning the lot of them to non-existence.

When he and his queen found this human threat to Feeder survival, O'Farrell would offer the criminal up to Her, so that they could make a bacchanal of his destruction.

Probing the top shelf of the shallow clothes closet, O'Farrell wrinkled his nose as a threadbare set of purple panties stiff in the crotch with menstrual blood tumbled down on his face. Now hungry. Now horny. He realised his faulty memory had left him unable to visualise Miranda's weathered face. Why exactly had he killed her again?

And according to the policeman's union, wasn't he overdue for his mandatory meal break?

XVI

*C*alie floated above the earth, a shuddering wraith. Her skin waited patiently below, softly crackling with black ether, a guardian field of stupid energy that house-sat for her ancient, many-spiked and hundred-roomed soul while it went roaming, to seek the satori of information, the brute power of enlightenment. A glimpse at the exact weave of nature's massive skein.

This was also when the death goddess indulged in subtle hypnagogic manipulation of her various prey, invading their dreams with restless visions and breathy suggestions. When Calie rode the skies, babies woke crying for no reason; old wives shifted restlessly next to their husbands, dreaming they were young and soft and being consumed cunt and soul by a small, dark, hungry thing; mothers woke abruptly with tears in their eyes, reminded of suicided daughters.

Tonight, though, Calie's soul drifted distractedly, garlanded with the black poppies of a lazy dream time. Victim rather than predator: engulfed by visions of her new fascination, her potential toy, her lover, her succulent gourmet meal. Mistress Medusa, Mary Ellen Masters, little pawn, little saint.

And an exquisite little fuck, she imagined.

Weren't the saints famous for that particular talent? Notorious stories were passed around the infernal races of the triumphant pleasures to be earned by possessing the ultimate submissive: one of the Enemy's wretched, misery-loving martyrs, sanctified to the point of being too weak to even protest against the tortures of the wicked.

Saints. From all the stories, she figured them to be like little schoolgirls, ignorant and fearful, terrified to be introduced to the true pleasures of the flesh.

Calie had never met and therefore never tasted a saint directly touched by God. She had settled for a string of priests and nuns in the Greek Isles, a Monsignor in Paris, a few rabbis in Brooklin Heights. Teaching them the truth even as she drained them, about the truly fleeting nature of goodness, and the fragile illusion of freedom. Snuffing them with the pleasures of damnation.

And not a one of these holy men had ever fought back. Despite the myths of dragonslayers and virgin Amazons, Calie had never encountered any warrior saints among the humans. The blessed were pathetic and cowardly; the few others that had sought to defy her will over the centuries were alone and helpless, no greater power at their side or informing them.

Not that she was not aware of the destruction she courted through her cavalier torture and consumption of God's favourite cattle.

She had heard of the angels, of course, in their many ranks and forms, but still of one race, a people at His command that was to a Feeder such as her what she was to a human. What a human was to a cow. Even the humans had stories of them, though their limited perceptions and prejudice insisted on reducing the fearsome creatures to feathery-winged cherubs and the like.

Let the angels come and take me. To ancient, jaded Calie, existence was little beyond a desultory, endless joke. She did not know whether she was immortal or merely long-lived, but either way, she was a lonely, crossbred mule, sick of the burden of thought and animation.

She imagined herself washed in the merciless anger of an angel of the Lord. Great, inscrutable beings who strode through a different dimension, a flatter earth, their throats vibrating at an impossible rate, their huge black wings rustling, ever ready to visit the torments of God's vengeful destruction upon infernal carrion and criminals from birth such as herself.

Calie floated onwards through her rising visions: Mary Ellen as slaughtered infant, Mary Ellen as split-open fruit. Rotating helixes lazily tumbled over themselves, the secret of Mary Ellen's DNA. God's recipe for a martyr, if you were to heed the human belief that He had some eternal plan.

The glint from Mary Ellen's pale blue eyes now illuminated a terrifying vision of the most savage of God's bully boys, a legendary figure of whom she'd heard many bloody tales. Called Michael by Rome, Mika'il by the wild-eyed Muslims in the desert; Michael of the Flames, chief of the archangels, lord of the order of virtues, like unto God himself and just as proud and impassive, who through angelic privilege at his whim would rape and dismember any of the abandoned, infernal races he happened upon, with the excuse that it was they who preyed upon the sacred lambs, the anointed beloved who were by nature to dragon, vampire, Lamia, and werewolf food and chattel.

Such hypocrisy. Judging by many of the stories she had heard, the humans weren't held in any higher regard by the often querulous angelic hosts, either. God wanted his herd of sheep conserved, and the angels carried out His will. It didn't mean they liked it.

As her visions began to coalesce and resolve, Calie could feel herself going vague; it seemed to be time to return to her body. Rather than the usual, calm seeping-in feeling, however, the process was jarring and painful; she imagined that her flesh was spreading in boiling patches across her outraged nerve clusters.

In a moment, she was whole, and knew something was wrong: she was not where she had lain down to travel. She had woken from her dream into a nightmare.

Standing before her was the terrible apparition of Michael himself, the merciless destroyer of Babylon. A forest of dripping metal and concrete trapped her close to him. She could not see the night sky; his wings were great and emerald green, receding so far off into the darkness that the horizon was obscured.

Creaking like great engines, his wings now beat the air so hard that embers kicked up from the suddenly burning metal were driven with gale force into her morbid flesh, hollowing out divots that as she held up her hands in protection she could now see resembled the cigarette burns she would leave on the arms of the masochists who came before her on their knees at the dungeon.

As he came closer she saw that he was covered with saffron hairs, each of them containing countless tiny faces, mouths all working in unison to produce a painful buzz, a sound that insinuated itself in the back of her neck, where wires were pulled that now spastically yanked her limbs this way and that.

The air was damp and metallic with ozone, and the prickling of static electricity rippled mockingly through her thighs. Gazing down, she saw that Michael had sprouted a huge, flaming penis, and she was skewered on it...though she didn't feel a thing ...How odd, to be fucked and not feel it ...especially when her rape was by the nemesis himself, supposedly the greatest power of all ...She continued to drift through the night sky weightlessly, and thought of Mary Ellen's unique perfume, with its slight hint of the brooding scent of angels. And came, in a series of devastating orgasms that lasted until just before dawn.

Despite the breeze from the crack in one of the bedroom window's brittle old panes, Mary Ellen was aroused by the rich stink of her own sweat.

She had lost her dream an instant after her eyes snapped open, but was left with a provocative impression of Lady Calie, the monster who had been hired to be a mistress at the dungeon.

After their initial brush, Mary Ellen had steered clear of the slithering little demon. To everyone else, she knew, Lady Calie was an attractive Eurasian of indeterminate age, with long, dark kinky hair, and a flat, broad nose made inconsequential by an oversize, predator's slash of a mouth. Despite the epicanthic folds, her eyes were also riveting, two hazy, dark marbles, the iris crowding out nearly all of the white.

Calie was the sort who could load the most simple declaration with horrid levels of suggestion: "We should really do a session together sometime," delivered in her low, cautious monotone became an obscene flirtation, a suggestion of myriad demanding and unpleasant possibilities.

Living with a monster in your midst was a strange adjustment, Mary Ellen found. Despite the insinuations, Calie had made no overt threat to her. And the dungeon was, at this point, the only work Mary Ellen knew. If she had enough money, maybe she could flee …But where? Wasn't the whole world probably like this? Wasn't she at least safer where she knew people, where people knew her, where she knew to avoid the blind alleys and dark side streets?

So she had stepped into the breech, and after a week of being plagued by The Manager's insistent campaign and Calie's well-placed suggestions, Mary Ellen was going to enter a dungeon with the inhuman mistress. She knew one thing already: Axel's knife was coming with her. She would keep it near her, wave it around as if it were a toy to frighten whoever the supposedly excellent client was that Calie had scared up for their collaboration.

"He's a special client of mine, Mistress Medusa. A professional man, very staunch, very stubborn, simple but hearty tastes. You'll love digging into him," Calie had pitched her.

"I think we'd make a great team, and I know he'd just love you to death, too," she'd added, smirking provocatively.

Hearing her voice in her head, Mary Ellen's dream came drifting back to her in shreds, seeping up from the twisted pillow supporting her skull: Calie in the throes of an awful passion, as if possessed. Calie skewered, on the most implacable cock imaginable.

Restless, Mary Ellen threw off the comforter and was shocked by the musk gathered between her legs. Guiltily, she rubbed a finger there, and brought it swiftly up to her nose, inhaling deeply but only once, her head pushing back against the pillow with the impact of her excitement.

It was almost like a crush, like a dance of seduction: nightmaring about that dusky and small, seductive little monster; and this afternoon would feature their vaunted and postponed collaboration. She knew the impetus for this joint venture was not financial, no matter what the excuses her fellow mistress made.

Calie wanted time alone with her. Calie wanted her. She could tell. That was the truth of it, terrifying yet provocative; this inhuman thing was attracted to something about Mary Ellen, who had long thought herself past being moved at offered the role of object of obsession, of lust or affection. The domination business had burnt that out of her, right down to ash.

There was a dangerous voice surfacing in Mary Ellen's head, however, a seductive drawl she remembered from her wild 20s, when it would insist to her that knowledge was supreme, experience was everything. To not know how something felt was to be lessened. So why shouldn't she go along with Lady Calie's program to an extent, just to see. To learn. To feel. Something new.

The truth was that Mary Ellen hadn't really felt much for a long time now, since way before she had been granted her burdensome gift of this hellishly divine vision. Love was an abstract concept, a rumour, a theorem she had missed on her college calculus test. And mere sex, even the once-exotic gardens of S/M, had paled into such boring predictability that there was indeed a suppressed hunger that had been bubbling within her since before this whole mad ride had started; a desire to know something she had never known before. Even if it meant her destruction.

Mary Ellen fell back to sleep with That Voice for company.

Somewhere just after dawn, seemingly only an instant later, the clock radio began braying the local heavy metal station. One of their more irritating, constantly chuckling DJs. Wiping the sleep from her eyes and listening to the bones in her neck creak, she wondered for the hundredth time if the radio announcer really was a stupid surfer from California or if that was just what demographics demanded he be. He was probably an old hippie who didn't even own a pair of leather trousers or a skateboard.

She punched the alarm off, and fell back into a thick, drugged stupor.

When she woke again, it was already eleven sixteen. The session was at one. Barely time for a hurried shower, half a cup of strawberry yoghurt and a stale bialy from two days before that she found crumpled in wax paper at the back of the refrigerator.

The apartment was blessedly silent, since she had disconnected her private client line a week ago. It was not like she had been answering it any longer; when it filled up with messages, she erased them without checking. She had no desire to look upon the tragic corps of inveterate wankers, mommy-lovers and hostile self-martyrs with the vivid clarity of her latest sense. Chewing the dry, tough unleavened bread, she pawed aside the vertical blinds and immediately regretted it. Refracting off the apartment window on the other side of the courtyard, a sunbeam drilled into her eyes. She blinked and let the tattered blinds fall back clattering. Felt faint and in that moment remembered her dreaming with alarming precision. Lady Calie naked, with razors neatly sunk half an inch apart in sine wave patterns over every inch of her flesh. Lady Calie taking Mary Ellen in her embrace, kissing her, taking her tongue between her impossibly sharp teeth and effortlessly slicing the tip off. There was no blood. Just a raw taste at the back of her throat.

Packing her duffel bag with a ripped pair of fishnet pantyhose, her personal piercing kit and a leather corset, Mary Ellen hesitated before stuffing Axel's knife at the bottom of the bag. Not that she truly expected Calie would do her any harm, at least not at the dungeon. She suspected there would be a much more complex seduction ritual involved than that.

As she shut her apartment door behind her and headed down the hall for the elevator bank, her boots muffled by the thick carpet, she shivered, and wondered shame-facedly whether in fear or anticipation.

XVII

Mary Ellen felt as if she were trapped in the most frustrating, sodden nightmare imaginable.

She offered a frozen smile and twisted the huge, rubbery nipple of the enormous, bad-smelling giant that Calie had used a dozen yards of her trademark neon-bright nylon cord to bind up.

Mary Ellen looked up into the rough, oversized and cruel features and offered her best professionally bland expression of seduction; even that cheap cartoon was difficult to manage under the circumstances. She was grateful for the countless sessions that had taught her to function in bizarre and difficult situations on robotic autopilot. The Manager called it professionalism. A therapist she had wasted a lot of money on had called it dissociation.

Dissociation had presented itself to her as the easiest tactic to prevent terror when she had discovered that Calie's special, 'fun' client was yet another creature materialised up out of The Black.

Though not the surreal vision that the dragon which had slain Axel had been, the towering creature Lady Calie had silkily introduced as Detective O'Farrell was certainly gross and menacing enough. He looked like an ogre; she had half expected the first words out of his mouth to be "*Fe fi fo fum...*"

Now scraping her nails against O'Farrell's naked, coarsely-haired thigh and shuddering at what filth might be collected under them, she considered bolting for the door.

But that could mean an immediate attack from the both of them. The situation was too vaguely defined for such a definitive action. She couldn't be absolutely sure that these two creatures had set her up neatly, luring her into their clutches in an appropriately-equipped chamber of torture where they could take their unclean pleasures and revenge upon her.

She didn't think Lady Calie would do such a thing — not yet, at least, not before the visibly yearning sex vampire had sampled the flavour of Mary Ellen's soul. Monster or not, she recognised the lust in the other female's eyes — it mirrored the obsession in many of her clients' furtive stares.

And could it be a horrible coincidence?

Perhaps they could be toying with her. Could they be honestly ignorant of whom — no, make that *what* — she was metamorphosing into?

Feeling Calie's scrutiny from across the dungeon, she sensed that although throwing her together with this gruesome brute had been a conniving experiment on the small, wicked thing's part, the other dominatrix wasn't aware of the true drama of the situation. She didn't know that Mary Ellen recognised the bound giant before her for what he was.

"Would you like to clamp those nipples, Mistress? They seem to be asking for it," inquired Lady Calie, proffering two sets of surgical clamps that boasted gleaming, stainless steel teeth.

"Indeed I would, thank you very much," Mary Ellen

answered boldly, accepting the instruments and roughly closing them just at the tip of Detective O'Farrell's nipples. Where they would hurt the most.

So these things weren't omniscient. True, they did seem to boast a level of brute perception human beings didn't. But since Christmas Eve, so did Mary Ellen. As she had learned with the dragon, the night stalkers were not indestructible. And, though the thought of that hungry angel rising from behind the burning building disturbed her, there were higher powers than these base cartoons of amoral hunger, these predators who seemed devoted to nothing but the sadistic fulfilment of the hunt.

"I think from the expression on Detective O'Farrell's face, you've struck a nerve, Mistress Medusa," Calie announced, smugly clamping her small but powerful fist around the ogre's oversize ball sac. The wattled flesh overflowed her grip extravagantly, so that her razor tip talons were sunk so deeply they were out of sight. The unfortunate beast threw back his head and let loose a moan that was just short of a normal man's bellow. Mary Ellen resisted the urge to grin, for fear of inciting their client to mayhem.

Before this jarring, heart-palpitating moment, she had been practically on the verge of adjusting to her new reality. After the flames of her initial terror dwindled to a less blistering intensity, Mary Ellen had begun to examine her encounters with these otherworldly creatures that seemed to infest the New York City she had known all her life, transforming it into a jungle more thick with dangerous species and a finely-tuned predatory ecosystem than the wilds of the Amazon which she had seen on the Discovery Channel.

These hungry creatures were all potentially deadly, and no matter their various masquerades, they were not human. But unlike that radiant force which had visited her in the next dungeon on Christmas Eve, a mere eight weeks back, or the callous angel that two weeks ago had nearly swept her off Second Avenue and up to heaven on the heaving wings of a celestial orgasm, they were made of nearly as mean a material as mankind, assuredly of this world.

Yes, as the dragon in the women's room had so ably demonstrated, they bled. And died, after awhile.

Mary Ellen wondered what colour Calie's life fluid was. Possibly a venomous green, she speculated. She was seized with a hateful need to find out; her flight or fight mechanism, trying to balance itself out under all this input.

As for the giant who now writhed beneath the spiked glove Calie casually drew across his belly, the golem whose great maw stunk abominably beneath a thin layer of mouthwash with the unspeakable rot and decay of a meat far richer than any Mary Ellen had ever smelled cooking, his blood was probably as red as hers. Though she imagined it dribbling out in a thick pudding, the beast would probably slap at it in confusion, and try to stuff it back in.

Mary Ellen suddenly felt high, the safe supreme rush of adrenaline from her fear now galvanising her. She stared at Calie in open contempt and amusement, struck by the ridiculousness of the moment. *Who were these pathetic, skulking things, to stalk* her? *Jackals, that's what they were, waiting to be driven off by the light of the righteous.*

Mary Ellen shook her head, disoriented by the alien voice that had just tried to pose as her own thoughts, intruding suddenly and without raising any alarm. Who was the righteous? Mary Ellen? And what light did she wield? Where was the dagger?

She retreated from the scene to lean against the bondage table where she had stowed her toy bag, as if she were stepping back for a bit of perspective on the work of art they were creating. She knew Lady Calie would appreciate the gesture.

Gripping the edge of a chair tightly, trying to look nonchalant to the now-provoked Calie, she couldn't believe that these leering monsters had for a moment seemed so inconsequential, so easy to sweep away.

"Mistress, our toy seems a little bored. Perhaps he's the jaundiced sort. Or perhaps I bore him. Do you have any ideas on how we might dissipate the poor thing's ennui?"

Calie spoke while weighing the ogre's nearly erect, massive cock in her hand, jiggling it as if it were a piece of raw meat. O'Farrell looked puzzled at Calie's vocabulary, but still squirmed his hips expectantly, hoping for more exquisite touches from his two hired tormentors. He seemed not to notice the clamps anymore.

A room illuminated itself in Mary Ellen's head. She gave Calie a triumphant smile.

"You know, Mistress, I *do* think I have just the thing."

Medusa turned to the black duffel bag full of toys and personal effects. Since returning to work she had taken to keeping it in the rooms with her during session. She felt safer with the bag around. That was where she kept Axel's dagger tucked away.

When O'Farrell saw the blade, his shock was palpable in the air.

"Oh look, my big old toy, your new mistress has found just the thing to teach you a few new tricks."

As Mary Ellen stepped forward, holding the knife to the tip of her nose so her features were bisected and purposeful, the ogre burst out into a reeking sweat, and looked frantically at Lady Calie, as if he had something he wanted to say.

Calie's laugh was a venomous froth.

"Could our big bad boy be afraid of sharp, metal things?"

Standing before him, Mary Ellen felt the heat off their captive's chest. Seeming of its own volition, the oversize blade now traced a series of twisting dance steps across the behemoth's chest, skittering against a pore here, lightly dashing through a thicket of coarse hair there.

His stupid features were a mask of terror, and his chest no longer heaved with his rancid breath, as Mary Ellen amused herself. She felt giddy with power. The beast really was frightened of her — and of Axel's blade.

Calie chuckled from behind her shoulder, and urged her on.

"You seem to have his attention now, Mistress. What are you going to do with it? I know he seems stupid, but he is quite capable of learning, if the lesson is reinforced strongly enough. Isn't that right, student?"

Calie stepped up to the bound giant and stretched up to capture a dollop of the sweat from his forehead, then wiping it from the crook of her finger with a dark, squarish tongue like that of some small, needle-toothed beast of the wild.

"Rather piquant. What have you been eating lately, Detective?" Calie inquired, giggling as if she had made a joke. Horribly, Mary Ellen suspected she understood the implication.

The rap at the door made everyone jump; the odorous giant stressed his bonds to the breaking point. An airy voice came from the other side of the door. Lady Marlena.

"Mistress Medusa! The Manager wants to see you."

Not quite believing that she would even toy such with this moment of unlikely salvation, Mary Ellen found herself gazing at Calie's inviting curves and tumbling hair as she blithely called back, "I'm in the middle of session, Lady Marlena!"

"I understand, Mistress Medusa. His apologies to the client and to Mistress Calie, but an emergency situation demands your immediate attention!"

Mary Ellen shook her head at Lady Calie, trying not to smirk with the exultation as her escape from this nest of perverse evil became imminent.

"Oh, tell the old bastard I'll be right there," Mary Ellen

scolded through the door, in mock anger. Calie stared at her in amazement and frustration, and the furnace of hatred from the bound giant flared with pure malevolence. Mary Ellen grabbed her bag from the bondage table and slid the blade back in, and then kept the bag dangling from her fingers, as if she were being absent-minded. The blade would stay in her hands. She could see how it frightened O'Farrell.

And though Calie's intentions still were not certain, there was now no doubt as to how this great, vicious thing with flesh on its breath meant to end this session. Whether he had known of her unique gift to begin with or not, Axel's knife had indeed incited him.

"*Au revoir*, Mistress Medusa. Say goodbye to Mistress Medusa, Detective O'Farrell."

Detecting the ogre's low growl, Mary Ellen gratefully went to see The Manager, leaving these two inhuman beasts with only her half-nervous, half-triumphant smile.

XVIII

*t*he dull red iron door swung shut firmly behind her.
Mary Ellen drew the belt of her leather jacket tightly
around her waist so the winter wind could not come
creeping up her belly.

In her purse were two greasy, stained fifties, pressed on her
by The Manager. Normally, she would have never agreed to
go on a run for him. Not any more; since she had cleaned her
own act up, she found wallowing in the excessive sleaze of the
Lower East Side drug culture repugnant.

The brisk breeze enveloped her as she marched off into the
grey afternoon, towards Seventh Avenue, where she could
catch a downtown taxi. The bland white and rust concrete of
FIT cast anaemic shadows into the street; there were no students to be seen, driven into local coffee shops by the cold.

The one odd thing about her inadvertent rescue had been
The Manager's demeanour.

He had been oddly lucid and calm, hardly in the throes of

withdrawal. Yet he had insisted, with all apologies and grace, that the drug run must be made immediately.

She hadn't really argued. Instead she rebuked him for his habit at the same time he held her hand, whispering her chide since that runaway slut Alanna had been asleep on his lap.

He had not bothered to whisper, however, instead speaking in full, melodious inflections. Alanna didn't wake up, or even shift in her sleep. On her way out, Mary Ellen was surprised to notice that Odin, The Manager's mangy bird, was also asleep on its perch in the corner.

XIX

*t*he Manager started, rocked by the force of an escaping hallucination, a muffled dream that Medusa had been present in the room, that he had been in conversation with her.

The television set's oversize screen still danced silently with a constant flow of jerky cartoon images, tuned in to a cable channel devoted to nothing but twenty-four hours a day of primary colours and limited movement.

Odin rustled on his perch in the corner, spastically clutching the pitted wooden bar with his scaly feet, his feathers making metal pings as they brushed the bars of his cage. Darting his head toward his owner, the cockatoo puffed a concerned raspberry from between his pursed beak. His uneasy companion, The Manager's pet ferret, was nowhere to be seen, having evidently sought refuge behind one of the bookcases or in another of his regular hidey-holes.

A slight shift in her posture made The Manager aware of

Alanna's warm weight next to him. His latest protégée was a pleasingly touchy-feelie specimen, and though she didn't actually fuck him, the grimy ripeness of her drug-bloated, freckled face and the bony promise of the girlish hips beneath her baggy, low-riding jeans pleasantly provoked him. Especially when she would curl like some small furry thing around his waist or feet and sink into a braying snooze, her skull of brown curls against his leg but laid careful so as not to rest against the tender flesh surrounding his still open, still suppurating bullet wound, a hole of nearly six months vintage that refused to close. Even his quack doctor, the one who had sold him several prescription pads over the years, was demanding that he go to the hospital for tests, but The Manager was terrified that they wouldn't let him come back out with the calf and foot intact.

Alanna shifted again. He turned to see her sit abruptly up, back straight and eyes wide with something between fear and adoration. Her dingy t-shirt was crumpled around her high, pointy breasts, and she was digging her unclean feet nervously against the bunched-up bedspread at the bottom of the mattress.

"How did you do that?" she asked, her New Jersey drawl, usually so blithe with chemical-induced tranquillity, small and vibrant like a pigeon's coo.

"Uh," he responded, his tongue sluggish with a copper-flavoured coat that was accompanied by a slight stinging sensation, as if he had just licked the end of an exposed live wire.

Though she was obviously overwhelmed by something, Alanna's pug nose was wrinkled up in delight; making The Manager feel the warm embrace of relief. With the runaway's schizophrenia progressing as her ingestion of prescription tranquillisers grew more and more sporadic and her pilfering of his coke stash more frequent, her moods had become explosive and unpredictable. There was no telling what sort of statement or action might terrify or anger her; he had to be on constant guard.

But even though for some reason he couldn't remember the moment that had preceded this one, he now could safely assume he had done something right.

"Jus'…um…asleep a seck…und," he slurred, trying to cram the missing details of whatever state his body had just experienced into the comfortable explanation that he had been on the nod.

Nods, however, never left his body vibrant and tingling like this, the points of electricity between his toes and the tip of his head so…clean and focused. Though there was the hint of muscle tissue strain in the back of his neck, as well as in his fingers and anchoring his belly, overall he was basking in a state of extreme well-being. He felt better than he had in sometime. Since, come to think of it, the last time he had passionately fucked his vein with a warm hypo full of liquid nirvana. Which had been six years ago.

Since those days of total surrender, he had subsisted on the Program, a cold purgatory which nevertheless allowed him to function, after a fashion, and conduct his business. The cocaine was necessary because it was the only thing that chased away the cobwebs, though its numb grip sometimes conspired with the methadone to drag him down into ironic replicas of the very dope nods he had sought to free himself from in the first place.

Thinking about dope, he rubbed his mouth. His gums were tender against his upper dental plate, as if he had been grinding his jaw for two days straight — a habit he had acquired more than once, while experimenting with the adjustment of his drug flow. But episodes like that were stark for their unmerciful degree of clarity, a relentless low-level torment that painted each moment with endless and excruciating detail.

"You were blue fire, and you were gone," Alanna announced to him in a tone somewhere between accusation and accolade.

He looked down at her, and saw a childish innocence that should have been drowned by now with the drugs and her father's ravishments and the month spent as a house girl over at an East Side place run by the Mafia, swallowing the stubby cocks of unpleasant young lawyers willing to pay a little more to shiver with the tender sucklings of the half-way innocent young stuff.

Alanna was the classic sad case, a trouble magnet headed toward nothing but more of the same, and The Manager knew the drill all too well, despite the halting pangs of conscience that drove him to lecture her on the evils of drugs and promiscuity — even as he counted the sweaty dollars passed over to him from the garter of some eye-rolling employee who retreated as quickly as possible, or lingered if she was indeed one of the nose candy enthusiasts who was always hoping to be invited to stay and do a line.

Now though, Alanna seemed magically imbued with a restoration of the caul she had once told him had blanketed her in the womb, an unlined soul bright with its newness. The constant hue of madness behind her eyes had subsided, and The Manager perceived her, there on his bed, clad in nothing but dirty blue underwear and loose tank top, as a little girl receiving her first communion, perfectly pure and untouchable in her awed anticipation and delight.

"What do you mean, Alanna?" he wondered out loud, and the words came easier this time, the control of his vocal chords more sure and easy. Out of the corner of his eye he could see Yogi Bear was knotting his tie and waggling his eyebrows, while Boo-Boo looked up at him in adoration, waiting for the old picnic-basket hustler to explain his latest con.

"Every word was sweet. Candy-music, it kissed my throat,"

she whispered in a small voice, a loose, dreamy smile playing around her chubby little lips.

"Everything exploded in the nicest way, and I felt like we were hugging, even though I was way down here," she continued. She didn't seem at all surprised that The Manager needed to be informed of his own behaviour for the last few minutes.

"So calm, and safe. Protection from all bad. So huge; something in you and I knew it didn't love me, exactly, but I was its daughter, and it would watch out for me. Like Daddy said once. But no lies here. Only light."

The Manager wondered if Alanna was going to get too attached to him; he hadn't worked out for himself yet that the adulation he sought in his protégées was exactly what made him discard them.

He twisted against the headboard toward his bookshelf, seeking his stash; Lady Marlena had just made a run for him over an hour ago, and he was proud that he hadn't even dug into it once yet.

XX

O'Farrell was close to a berserker rage.

Not only did the stupid human slut who had taunted him with the very iron blade used to kill a Feeder slip from his grasp, but then, why *then*, when he had bellowed his wrath and frustration, there had been less than no sympathy forthcoming from Calie, his cold, diffident demon lover. Only an unexpected alarm, which she thought concealed by her amusement. Oh, but he could smell alarm. He had learned how in the cradle.

Not that the sleek domina wasn't putting up a properly imperious front.

"You can find some crack whore for supper, ogre. The woman is touched by the Enemy, and she is mine," Calie informed him, as he hopped on one foot, tugging his oversize pants back on.

"She's an enemy to us both!" he roared back. She brought the edge of her palm to her lips, shushing him.

"Lower your voice, you stupid brute, we're not alone here. There's a whole menagerie of humans in this place!"

"So what if there is! I could murder them all, and make it look like a drug killing," O'Farrell hissed at Calie as she went about the business of cleaning up the dungeon, winding the forty feet of rope that had been used to create a spider web about him. He hopped around on one huge foot, pulling his trousers up.

"You could. If I were to let you."

Losing his balance, he nearly fell over. When his encumbered foot sought purchase, he felt one of the inseams of his trousers tear.

O'Farrell couldn't believe it. Calie, his death goddess, was standing between him and what was, by Feeder nature and right of the hunt, his food. *Their* food.

She stood there stone-faced, looping the rope around her elbow, her compact curves revealed and enhanced by the black leather straps that crisscrossed her waist and came up between the inside of her thighs, covering her crotch but exposing the hard cheeks of her ass. Anger and lust fused within him in a near-unbearable white-hot fountain.

Sensing his imminent loss of control, Calie stalked forward and threw the coils of rope around his neck, drawing his face down to hers. As she drew the coils tighter, her supernatural strength told by the cool black spots of oxygen deprivation that presently exploded in his brain, dousing the flame of his anger, she kissed him deeply, seeking his tongue with her teeth, nipping at it lightly, tugging at it just enough to make him wince.

Distracted from his racial hatred for Medusa, his huge hands came around Calie, engulfing her bare rear in a surprisingly delicate grip.

In acknowledgement, she bit down on the end of his

tongue, and he momentarily swooned, even as his mouth filled with a warm wetness that she quickly drained off.

Still holding the rope tightly around his neck, she reared back, so he could see her sharp, monumental features, impassive with her will. Her almond eyes were filled with blood, obscuring the pupils. Her lower lip was extra-crimson with the stain of his life force.

"Mistress Medusa will not be a problem. I will see that she never slays another Feeder. Do you not trust your Mistress, fool?"

O'Farrell growled, prompting Calie to then draw her noose to the point where the huge ogre had no breath at all left to protest with.

Eyes bulging, massive cock now having burst the zipper of his pants, he nodded. Once. Calie relaxed her grip, but before he could tumble down to snuffle in her crotch, as was his wont at moments like this, she grabbed his chin and spat his own blood back into his mouth. Now mixed with her venom, which boasted highly-addictive properties. Then she let him root as he would between her legs with his slavering, blubbery lips.

After all this time, she knew the proper equations of punishment and reward, after all.

"That's it, my sweet. Soothe yourself with my wine."

She relaxed herself and commanded the release of a wash of bubbling, acidic urine into O'Farrell's gulping mouth. The noises were obscene.

XXI

Squeezed back into his oversized, battered unmarked car, his fresh orgasm now nothing more than an extra rank bouquet between his legs and the taste of his mistress's blood and piss sour on his tongue, O'Farrell gripped the tiny wheel and stared ahead, waiting to pull into traffic as he planned Mistress Medusa's destruction.

Despite Calie's assurances, which he saw through as evidence of her own lust and fascination with the human woman, Medusa could not be allowed to walk around, bearing as she did the secret of iron. Having used it once, she would again. As a cop, he knew that much; once these humans discovered how easy killing truly was, they rarely saw reason to stop with just one exercise.

There were measures that had to be taken. Order in the tribe must be kept, after all. Humans were to be stalked, not feared. Even if it was at the price of his outlaw mistress's wrath, he would set matters right. Her anger would subside, and if not, well...sometimes Feeders fed upon each other.

Being a cop; being an ogre. Sometimes there wasn't much difference. It was all about following the rules, keeping the secrets. Like the secret of iron. Thinking of the blade, somehow carved with the ancient sigils of protection, he shuddered. He needed back-up.

He thought of the wolf he knew, who lived in a cardboard box under the Brooklyn Bridge. And the little black schoolgirl, who if he hadn't known better would have thought upon first glance a treat sweet enough to savour for days. That is if she hadn't have been one of those treacherous fuck demons that preyed on human and ogre alike, that joyfully sapped your essence while they sat astride you in your sleep, milking you with their terrible muscles as if you were a cow.

Medusa would be at the Black Ball, he expected. The two of them had talked about it during the session, as if he weren't even there. That would be the place; he knew the Marshall Hotel, with its many dungeon-like basement rooms. Places where quickly stifled screams would not ring even as far as the elevator bank. He had investigated a murder there once; not one of his own.

Trying to drive through the congested Midtown evening traffic, his concentration was being diverted. But he made a mighty attempt to picture it, anyway, in his mind: All his marshalled forces, their lines of descent intersecting with the Black Ball as the central point, where not even fearsome Calie would stand in the way of Feeder justice, a blow against both the hated humans and perpetually angry old Wotan One-Eye.

XXII

"Ladies, gentlemen, and every rank in between, the Black Ball now takes great pleasure in introducing to you: the one, the only, the fabulous *Mademoiselle Ferret,*" announced Mistress Candida.

Alexis and Candida stood together on the club stage, two mismatched studies in feminine vanity. Candida was clad in an elaborate tunic of chain mail and leather with a matching head piece that made her look vaguely like Joan of Arc, while the diminutive Alexis, clutching the Xeroxed program, wore a crisp vinyl jumpsuit and extravagantly high spiked-heel boots that still fell short of bringing her to eye level with her partner.

Mary Ellen stood a few rows back from the foot of the stage, arms crossed, three dollars worth of plastic cup and ginger ale in one hand. Alexis and Candida, feared and hated by most of the other mistresses in New York City. Infamous for their endless machinations and grudges. They took pride not only in being scandalous, but in their dark reputation.

Mary Ellen shook her head, that such petty soap opera had once held any attraction to her at all. She was embroiled in much more grand drama now; true life or death scenarios. She wondered when Lady Calie would materialise; it was inevitable, of course. When Mary Ellen had admitted during their session with that big brute that she was attending the Ball, the delight in her infernal suitor's eyes had been immediate.

Mademoiselle Ferret, the self-proclaimed human vampire, took the club stage in her signature red-drenched wedding dress, its rumpled train brushing the splintered steps. An awkward transvestite stagehand traipsed out on vintage platform heels and set a silver serving tray laden with various implements on the front of the stage.

Mademoiselle Ferret took the mike and launched immediately into her vaudeville act from hell.

"Well howdy-do, all you Black Ballers. I've balled a few blacks myself, you know. In the '70s, when you could make off with their velour pimp hats while they were sleeping. I've got quite a collection."

Mary Ellen had seen her perform around town during the last year, both at the fetish clubs and down in the artier East Village joints; she sometime stripped at a SoHo lap-dancing joint as well.

She was a weird sight, indeed, even in light of Mary Ellen's initiation into this new world of unearthly spectacle.

"But I'm sure you didn't come here tonight to hear about my venereal history. Unless you're with the press, of course. Now talk about *vampires*..."

Yes, Mademoiselle Ferret with her dentally-bonded fangs, her pruned ears and flat black hair. Mademoiselle Ferret, who once planned to be fisted on stage by a midget stationed underneath that stained dress, only to be thwarted by the paucity of hardcore dwarfs available these days in New York

City. Poor dejected thing had to settle for a diminutive young anarchist squatter instead.

That she was so undeniably human was what made her casual decadence singular; it was the kind of extravagant, self-belittling extrapolation that only humanity could manage. Mademoiselle Ferret, through surgery and force of will, had made herself the mechanical bride to the end times, the bleakly camp Madonna to the birth of the next century, the one after history's diminish. "You don't say, Charles," was her signature remark, delivered in an ice-hot drawl, all droll and fake-bored.

Mary Ellen understood the impulse. Before everything changed, Mary Ellen had been as fascinated with vampires as anyone else in American society was these days.

You always wanted to believe that the most noble, the most damned creature of them all, red jester of our Saturday matinee and comic book reveries, might in some sort of incarnation really exist. Perhaps because proof of the devil is proof of God; perhaps because the blood-drinker is the most sybaritic, primitive thing imaginable, blessed with a simple hunger and cursed with tangled consequences.

But now Mary Ellen had more proof than she could have ever conceived of both God and the devil, or at least his children, and would have just as well gone without, thank you very much, Fate.

That was why she was no longer so provoked by this false succubus on the stage, with her slim, muscular dancer's build and her broad, feral Roman features. She was no more than a vacuum of self-recreation, a monument to the human ability to bend the flesh to the ego's will,

"Let's see if we can get this right tonight, get the needle into the vein, get the flow going nice and thick. These damn veins. I just got out of rehab and can't do a thing with them,"

Mademoiselle Ferret drawled. The crowd clapped, whistled and cheered.

At the Ball tonight there was a real thirst in the air, the kind of thirst that in other, more innocent times religion would have quenched; a little mild self-flagellation, an hour or two on your knees. But this was this crowd's religion going on here, a church of self-veneration, of wild decoration, of pressing fingertips up against the warm wall dividing birth from waste while hungering for the flavour of both. Mary Ellen remembered when she had belonged.

"Well, I could go on, but I'd rather be known as a ... sanguine kind of girl," Mademoiselle Ferret confided. Sensing the crowd's need, flattered to be their priestess, she whipped out a rubber hose from the folds of her dress and tied off her left arm.

A hypo shunt secured from the silver tray plunged into her main vein, was screwed into the blue threading beneath the flesh with a stiffly casual effort. Eyes sparkling and smile rictusing as if she were in the throes of a Carol Burnett routine, she allowed the first few tentative spurts to fall like red semen across the pale chiffon bustle of her dress.

Satisfied, her right hand closed around a crystal glass perched on the silver tray, swooped it up in a reverse 90-degree angle to the descending arc of her blood. An action performed with the grace of a hand model on a blandly upscale television commercial for the pleasures of self-mutilation.

The glass filled quickly, the vibrating crimson energy splashing the sides and drooling back down to collect in an ever-mounting pool, hypnotising the audience with its sultry gleam.

She transferred the filled vessel to her left hand and removed the shunt. The vein continued to spurt erratically until the wound clotted over. Then, her eyes betraying a sainted state of pure, hermetic self-obsession that rolled like light down glass into a pyrotechnic need for attention, for adoration, to generate fear and lust that she could either harvest or dance away from laughing, she drank.

Every throat in the house was suddenly parched, cursed with a thirst that the gassy beer on tap at the bar, the watery vodka-oranges, the thin colas couldn't quench. Mary Ellen sensed a collective thirst for the kind of orgasm that starts at the tongue and explodes in the belly, shock waves turning cocks engorged and turgid and pussies slick with goo.

"Now that," Mademoiselle Ferret announced, "was *vampire* masturbation."

The crowd cheered as she descended among them, gathering her gown so the tribal tattoo on her calf sinuously darted forward as if toward some newer prey.

Alexis and Candida now came forward to congratulate her, though their ginger embraces avoided the wet spots on Mademoiselle's freshly stained gown.

Once Mary Ellen would have been thrilled; now she was numbed. Slightly stupid, egotistical children at play, was all these supposedly glamorous women were, comically engaged in their desperate attempts at decadence. Their efforts were limp and ineffectual in light of the existence of those truly merciless societies that had lately revealed themselves to Mary Ellen.

What were the "dangerous" dwellers on New York's famously treacherous S/M scene to the monsters from the Black that walked among them? Just impudent children playing dress-up.

She wandered among the spoiled, bickering knots of gaudy children, one of them but not of them. As the party dragged onward, each second was a cold tableau, each minute a test of endurance, each half-hour a proof of the enduring human spirit. All the while she waited for the sight of Lady Calie, appalled at herself for her desire.

She witnessed decadent tomfoolery in abundance while she

waited. Paid mistresses scrawled "slut" in lipstick across pink-frocked businessmen's hairy fat-man breasts. Ungainly social climbers from New Jersey swooped about in thousands of dollars worth of exotic clothing meant to provide entrance into the fabled secret society of pleasure.

At least unlike at the usual fetish events, Mary Ellen was not continuously approached by desperate, driven and lonely men. That was when Mary Ellen felt the most like a whore, and a dishonest one, at that.

No, this elegant soirée was socially engineered to be upscale, heavily advertised in all the right places; Page Six of *The Post*, the Internet; *Screw* magazine. Heavily populated by mostly heterosexual couples and the always trolling contingent of professional dominas, it reeked of attitude, the confusion of desire for orgasm and the desire for power. Something a bit more complex and diseased than the interaction at the public clubs.

Occasionally Mary Ellen felt sexy in her soft leather scoop-front black yoke skirt and tight leather bra; she luxuriated in the tickle of her long black hair against her white shoulders, and when she screwed her blue eyes shut, the endlessly throbbing house music massaged her thighs something like the blood pulse of an insistent cock inside her. She had worn her favourite cross tonight, the silver one made out of the squeezed and elongated form of a woman. She knew it drew attention to the valley down the centre of her generous, still reasonably firm chest.

She had also strapped on a fancy tooled leather shoulder holster, in which she had sheathed Axel's dagger. She had seen how it frightened and agitated the ogre, and its weight just above her hip made her feel more confident. At least somewhat less than naked and helpless.

As the anonymous music throbbed on endlessly until her flesh began to go numb, she took census of all the mainstays of the underground scene that were here. That incestuous, cut-throat world was where she had spent the most vivacious years of her life; and here were the actors in that black comedy: Her bitchy, conniving competitors as well as the occasional sympathiser; her former employers, cultured pimps one and all. Her sycophantic worshippers, and her nervous clientele; who would never think of bringing their wives here. Even an ex-boyfriend of sorts, with whom she'd had a tumultuous sadomasochistic affair, hunkered over the bar, slumping in the embrace of his beloved Jack-and-a-Bud.

Mary Ellen felt a twinge of empathy and remorse at the sight of him; it startled her, to actually feel one of the old emotions, something besides fear, shock or nothing at all.

He had written her the most complex love sonnets she could ever imagine, and even published them in her honour. Then his roving eye had been caught by an eighteen-year-old mistress who also worked for The Manager. A wild, bad-tempered little Mexican girl who had grown up without a father, she had cuckolded him and finally slashed him with a kitchen knife when she suspected he was seeing Mary Ellen again. Now he stayed away from women altogether; she had heard. By the fresh scars on his bare arms, Mary Ellen thought he must into self-mutilation, then.

She saw Athena, seeming none the worse for wear after her copulation with the Coyote god: standing by the bar with one violet high heel dug into the back of a man in a tuxedo who was crouched at her feet. Since that night, Mary Ellen had found that with some distance the crazy, unpredictable energy of Athena's ritual and its unforeseen result was not so frightening. Maybe there really were some answers there; if she could communicate again with the Coyote spirit, the only apparition so far that had shown neither malevolence nor disregard.

Mary Ellen started weaving her way across the dance floor towards Athena and her date. An instant later, the crowd parted to disgorge Lady Calie directly in front of her, as if from nowhere.

She was dressed in a black jumpsuit made out of some sort of leather that had a gleaming, alligator-like texture to it. A series of narrow belts that were part of the suit formed a martial corset around her middle, pulling the material tightly against her small breasts, and similar straps on the thighs and down the sleeves crossed each other in longer, curving X figures that emphasised the quick, sharp movements of her hands. A zipper that ran halfway down the chest was tugged all the way shut, so that the only flesh in evidence were Calie's hands and face. Her hair had been painstakingly curled and primped so that it tumbled over her shoulders and back like a mass of agitated black snakes. She looked like an ornately evil oriental doll.

She smiled at Mary Ellen's consternation over being ambushed, and gestured for her to lean down so she could speak into her ear, and be heard over the music. Her cool breath tickled Mary Ellen's ear, projecting a voice rippling in an unnatural register that made every word clearly discernible.

"I hope I didn't frighten you. My entrances do tend to catch people off guard."

In the midst of her silky insinuations, Lady Calie frowned at the sight of Axel's blade resting on Mary Ellen's hip.

"Nice accessorising," she announced, colouring the two words with equal hues of condescension, disapproval and discomfort. To Mary Ellen, Calie's reaction was confirmation that she had made the right choice, wearing the blade. Axel was starting to take on saint-like proportions to her.

"Do you like it? Your client didn't seem to care for the way it felt."

Lady Calie smirked conspiratorially.

"O'Farrell is a crass and unsubtle fool; he's just one of my favourite animals, that's all. You have nothing to worry about from him."

"At least not as long as you say so, right?" Mary Ellen was irritated by Calie's arrogance, even if she probably was telling the truth. "But of course, that still leaves the problem of what I might have to fear from *you*."

A genuine expression of hurt fluttered across that otherwise cold mask.

"I suspect that you know what I am. That doesn't mean you know who I am," came Lady Calie's measured tones. Her expression began to subtly transform, like the distant shift of atmospheric fronts. Mary Ellen felt suddenly warm, as if basking in a tropical radiance.

"Have you ever been with an older woman before, little Mistress Medusa? Your great-grandmother was a young girl when I was old. Well-preserved, aren't I?"

Mary Ellen was taken aback by the deliberate bluntness of the other domina's approach. She gathered her composure and drawled a reply.

"The term 'woman' implies that you're human. Like you said, I can see you for what you are. And I'm not afraid of you."

And amazingly, she wasn't. By betraying her desire for Mary Ellen, Lady Calie was less uncanny, more of a predictable factor. Mary Ellen had years of experience dealing with suitors, stalkers and snake-oil salesmen. Even before she had taken the vows to become one of the corps of predatory nuns who lived off the tormented needs and lusts of New York City's more well-heeled male population, there had been a regular stream of supplicants. Some begging, some blustering; all after the same thing. Her. All of them thinking she should be flattered.

Lady Calie stood there before her, eyebrows knit, teething

her full bottom lip. Woefully close to human.

"I wasn't suggesting you should be, Mary Ellen. Why should you be afraid of my love? Can't you see it's a more fabulous gift than any you'll ever be offered? You delight my senses. You command my attention. I need to know you, touch you, feel your touch. I offer you pleasure, not fear. You'll be safe, with me."

Until the sad, dreary day I'm through with you. Mary Ellen heard Calie's thought as if it had been spoken. So that was the way it was. There would have to be a way to play this out and save her skin.

Lady Calie said something that Mary Ellen couldn't hear. Glancing into her eyes, she saw that the Asian was staring past her shoulder, into the crowd.

Mary Ellen turned to see the object of her suitor's consternation. A pretty black girl in a schoolgirl uniform; she looked young enough to be legitimately dressed in plaid skirt and white blouse. For a second, Mary Ellen imagined the nubile little creature had somehow wandered into the party on the way home from studying late at the library. More likely a submissive at one of the houses, a college girl earning tuition and cocaine money.

This time Lady Calie's words were quite clear.

"That little wench. Gone hunting a bit out of her keep, hasn't she?"

Calie put a gentle hand on Mary Ellen's bicep, stroking it with her knuckles. It was all Mary Ellen could do not to shiver at the sudden tingle of black energy.

"Wait here, Mistress Medusa. I see a party crasher who needs to be shown the door. Someone you in particular might have found undesirable. But wait for me; there's still so much more to say."

Mary Ellen started to speak, but Lady Calie had disappeared into the crowd so quickly it was as if she had turned sideways and vanished into some fifth dimension.

Standing stupidly in the middle of the ballroom floor for a moment, she decided to complete her interrupted journey to the bar. Athena was no longer there. Gone off to one of the more private playrooms, perhaps, with that leashed business-man crawling behind her. Still, one stiff shot might be appropriate. Obviously Lady Calie was going to be persistent. To head off an ugly end, some plan had to be devised. She stroked the hilt of Axel's blade, wondering what she could do if it came to that.

Shouldering her way past a sot in a tuxedo who was trying to charm a middle-aged woman gaunt in head-to-toe black rubber, Mary Ellen found a handhold on the bar to anchor herself to and catch the overburdened bartender's attention.

Someone jostled her; a glancing blow but she nearly fell forward against the edge of the bar. She twisted around, ready to let loose a withering glare.

Detective Mickey O'Farrell loomed over her, straining the shoulders of an ugly trench coat. He blocked out much of the club's already dimmed lights. Mary Ellen put her hand to her waist for the iron blade; maybe it would get him to back off a few feet so that she could make a run for it.

Lady Calie's ogre grinned down at her, Axel's dagger clenched in its fist.

"You're busted," he said.

XXIII

*H*e had that arrogant little human bitch now.

Despite Lady Calie's interference, in five minutes the problem of her existence would be solved. This human slayer of Feeders would be so much freshly-prepared raw meat. Perhaps when his task was done his mistress would return to her senses, and see the bitch had been much too dangerous to toy with.

O'Farrell would not acknowledge to himself that jealousy had influenced his decision that Mistress Medusa had to be executed.

He felt the heavy weight of the dagger bouncing against his thigh, and was glad for the thick lining of his weathered overcoat; though iron was not the instant anathema to his kind that it was to more rare-blooded Feeders — such as Lady Calie, shouldn't she be *grateful?* — prolonged exposure would result in an unpleasant allergic reaction.

Lady Calie had to understand.

He had watched from a shadowy alcove, squeezed awkwardly behind a tiny cocktail table, as his mistress had eagerly sought out Medusa in the crowd. Waiting patiently for his plan to fall into place, he indulged in appetite-provoking, cock-thickening daydreams about some of the women walking by him. There were so many attractive morsels milling about, so alluringly packaged, O'Farrell felt as if he were confronted with a candy store window and, like a child, he did indeed want to eat them all up.

When Calie and Medusa met, he'd sat forward, now fully erect with the excitement of blood soon to be spilled. The pair chatted for a full minute, and O'Farrell grew impatient, heart hot with anger. Where was that little Feeder bitch?

Then she appeared, on the other side of the ballroom floor. Looking like the picture of misplaced innocence to the unwitting human audience that surrounded her, gazing variously in disdain and lustful appreciation.

But not to Lady Calie.

O'Farrell had introduced them once; the girl was a succubus he'd met while investigating her uncle's death; one look at the desiccated, pop-eyed bastard, lying on his blood-soaked cot in a small cubicle at the YMCA, great gouges scooped from his wrists, O'Farrell knew he had been an addict. When he'd visited the dead man's brother he'd figured out what the drug was as soon as her stepfather introduced Tyra.

A restless, wandering demon, she was fascinated by O'Farrell, having never had the opportunity to meet one of his kind during her century of travels in Africa and the Caribbean.

The physical aspect of their affair had not lasted past the first fuck; O'Farrell had been almost seduced by the sudden, rapturous weakness that overtook him when she climbed on top of him in the back of his car and squatted on his massive prick, easily engulfing it as if she were hollow inside.

Which was actually pretty much the case, as O'Farrell understood it. If he had let her milk him until he came, she would have been that much less hollow. For a little while. And he would have been stuffed in the drawer right next to the late, lecherous, pruned-out Uncle Bill.

Still, the haughtiness of her naked hunger had charmed him, and they had kept in touch, occasionally meeting at a coffee shop across the avenue from the Catholic high school Tyra attended. During one of those flirty bull sessions he had ended up telling her about Lady Calie, and the whole professional domination business in Manhattan.

Tyra had been fascinated, seeing it as a rich supply of food. She was tiring of playing the high school student; there was too much scrutiny of potential prey there. She would have liked a more anonymous killing ground.

Needless to say, Lady Calie had not been amused when O'Farrell had presented the cheeky young succubus.

Even now, the memory of the beating he had received after the chilly summit between the two female rivals made him flinch.

So of course the sight of Tyra would distract Lady Calie.

It had been beautiful, once it started; he felt something like a genius as he watched Calie dart away towards the intruding Feeder, and Medusa hesitate, then stride right over to the bar a few feet away from where he lurked as inconspicuously as he could.

It had been simple to roust her from the bar, and, one huge paw clenching her shoulder, direct her to the fire stairs and down here, to the guts of the building.

Though the huge boiler radiated an unpleasant degree of heat, O'Farrell did enjoy the grotto-like appearance of the basement room. It reminded him the slightest bit of home.

"So now you got me here, what are you going to do with me, Mr. Smellie?" Medusa taunted.

O'Farrell grunted in amusement. The bitch stood there, hip defiantly cocked even though her wrists were laid uncomfortably across it, manacled together with his police-issue cuffs.

He gingerly fished the blade out of his pocket, and dangled it in front of her nose.

"Evidence, ma'am. Have to take this back to the lab. Bet there's traces of blood on it. Bet you know something about it."

"Cut the shit, Sergeant Friday."

He wanted to correct her: Cannon. Sergeant Frank Cannon. But she wouldn't care; he could see that she was in a state of numb, hateful resignation. Her eyes cold and bright, her nose and the corner of one full lip twitching in contempt.

By Wotan, he would have preferred she show a little terror. After all, he was about to rend her limb from limb and swallow her raw, bloody heart.

He tossed the blade behind him. It made a dull *chuk* against the concrete wall.

"You have the right to remain silent. Anything you say can and will be used against you in a court of law."

O'Farrell's mouth went dry in anticipation of the fresh delicacy beating wildly in Medusa's chest. Just beneath the leather. Just beneath the skin. He brought his massive hands up before him, exhibiting them to Medusa. Turning them over. Nothing up the sleeve. Now watch this trick.

Stupidly, he observed his own hands spasm, fingers clutching toward the tufted palms. The result of a wave of pain which buzz-sawed through his nervous system, turning his knees to jelly and making his belly flip-flop with a wrenching nausea.

The source of the agony was a numb area in the centre of his back, where his spine should be. As he folded to the floor, he realised he couldn't feel his back at all.

He roared with anger and confusion, Mary Ellen forgotten, the matter of her execution put on the back burner. Dead case file.

"I always thought a big fellow like you needed more back-bone," came the familiar voice.

O'Farrell saw it all as if it were an evidence photo, or a TV show. Lady Calie standing over him, brandishing the iron dagger, her face, her fist, her hair, her curves, all conjured in several shades of red. Was she covered in gore, or had blood vessels in his head burst? There was definitely something wet on the blade; it gleamed under the direct light of the fly-specked bulb swinging above Calie's head, and something thick dribbled off the edge, headed for the floor. He thought he detected steam rising from her fist, where it wrapped around the handle of the iron dagger.

Gazing at her serenely cool expression, the ogre felt no anger; rather, he was consumed by grief over the betrayal. Didn't it matter, that it had all been for her?

"I took care of your little whore. It only took a moment, since I'm no puny, deluded human food, eager to be fucked out of existence at the sight of a pretty face. Did you think I wouldn't figure out you brought her here? Or why?"

O'Farrell's thoughts tumbled over themselves; things he wanted to say to her, meals he had consumed, orgasms that had consumed him. His mother's warm hand on his face, back in the mountains. Of Jorn Fafwuld's eyes when he had learned of his wife's death.

"I think you've become a liability, ogre. Disobeying me. Going behind my back. Doing things you know I won't like. I'm afraid we've reached the end of our relationship."

Suspecting from the way his arms and legs wouldn't answer his orders that they would be his last words, O'Farrell could-n't decide whether to say "*Fuck you, bitch*" or "*I love you*".

As it turned out, he could only roar in mindless panic and animal suffering, as Lady Calie began hacking away in great swathes with that cursed, trouble-making iron dagger, and he watched his viscera tumble out before him, the escaping steam scalding his cheeks as if he were shedding tears of fiery regret.

XXIV

the werewolf sensed a drastic change in the basement air, a brisk electricity slicing through the jungle of damp rot and must that had ruled the dark corridors moments ago. He could smell the sudden fear on the rats behind a riot of tumbled cardboard cartons, hear them scrabbling as they sought deeper refuge. A gentle shuffle of small feet against concrete prickled the fine hairs of his long ears, and he crouched low, growl vibrating deep in his chest as his bad eyesight strained, seeking the source of alarm. To his lupine vision, everything was in black and white, hazy shadows and stark quicksilver.

He spotted the form moving toward him, emerging from one of the closer offshoots of the basement catacombs beneath the old hotel.

A familiar sight: the succubus who stalked in the shape of a lithe Harlem schoolgirl, occasionally luring victims to the bushes in the same park he roamed day and night. Like him, one of the ogre's network of cohorts, connections and questionable associates.

The dark smooth carpet of her straightened long raven hair lay flat against her skull, and her large eyes seemed to spark right through the shadows that clustered deeply around them. Had she found their prey already, and fed?

He barked at her, a questioning challenge. Slowly, she looked up, and he realised that though it looked like her, the thing in front of him was not Tyra. The scent that came from his fellow Feeder was of something else yet again — something alien and threatening.

His primitive logic was confounded by the disparity. The odour that introduced itself to his flaring, leathery black nostrils was also vaguely familiar, and more than unsettling because of it.

He felt a primal fear swell in his belly at the sweet cloying promise of destruction, a fragrance complicated by the astringent tang of otherworldliness. A wind from the Other Place. The Place where the Ones came from, the Ones that made him into prey, when he was supposed to be the hunter, a nomad roaming the urban night, picking off humans who passed him off as just another homeless beggar with a filthy McDonald's soda cup dented by the odd quarter or penny. The Ones that cheated.

He had seen before his own eyes their vengeance; watched as the only bitch who had ever bore him a whelp was unceremoniously torn limb from limb by an angry black-wing, the bloody pieces raining down on Central Park as the previously clear summer night raged with a sudden electrical storm that turned every bristle on his body into a stiff arrow against smarting flesh.

She had been a fine one, his mate. Sinewy and powerful, a fortune-teller among the superstitious dark ones who dwelled in great numbers further North than the park when at rest. Even in her bare, smooth human skin she was breathtaking, never afraid to reveal her true nature to any of her weak, wide-eyed acolytes with one tooth-baring grin. They scuttled away and brought her gifts of food, money, crudely-made charms. It kept the two of them safe in a humble human-style den during the barren days of the month, when their spirits half-slumbered, yipping and growling in anticipation of the waxing of Goddess Luna that brought freedom and feast.

Together they had made that night, now thirty years ago, a hunter's moon that would have been savoured for decades to come. The prey was less fearful in those days, and easier found after dark on the quiet paths of embracing green, where custom and belief demanded meals be consumed. He had broken that tenet of his kind's simple religion many times since then, and grown used to the trespass. Let the black-wings take him when they would; to deny his nature would be worse damnation, and a betrayal to his ferocious mate's memory.

The slim, small succubus addressed him.

"Beast."

The voice was light and breathy, that of a young girl's, except for the brittle echo it carried, as if the syllable had been massaged by too many vocal chords.

The Feeder fell to all fours, great ears laid back and twitching.

XXV

——————

Mary Ellen fought nausea and a faint at the sight of the eviscerated giant, his stinking entrails blooming from his split-open belly like a huge, malevolent flower.

They were still, at least, not rising up in a pride of glistening vipers.

Distantly she heard the clatter of the blade against the concrete floor, and, feeling a sickening lurch of gravity as she tore her gaze from the gruesome corpse before her, looked straight into the eyes of her no-less-terrifying defender.

Calie stood over her, soft, small arms drenched in gore. She held out a crimson hand, palm still sizzling and bubbling where the iron pommel of the blade had touched, then drew it back in embarrassment when she saw Mary Ellen's look of horror.

"You see, Medusa, he didn't matter to me. Just one of the Gibborium, a brute toy to pass the time. You could be so much more. I don't want to hurt you. I just want to have you. Free you from your holy chains. You could come into the

Black, and be with me."

On the edge of madness, Mary Ellen felt an unexpected urge to succumb to Calie's desire; after all, so many times before in her life had she chosen that path, just to give herself over to the greater passion of an admirer, especially if he was attractive enough to reinforce her ever precarious self-image.

Calie was merely a soft, beautiful version of those hungry wolves, in their leather jackets, with their perfect hair and firm jaws, who came with no conscience or love, only to feed under the guise of caring, to suck her vitality down to the bone with empty promises of fidelity and infinity, of a true love that she knew was a particularly cruel chimera.

Calie so cleverly hid beneath the reassuring veil of Mary Ellen's own gender; it would be so easy, just a simple falling into; a melting, a mutual concupiscence that upon reaching maximum surface tensile strength would pop and intermingle every vital, previously private juice.

The banality of the party going on above them was such that Mary Ellen almost found herself hungry for Calie's embrace, no matter what the consequences.

"Don't you see, we're meant for each other, little martyr. Let me give you my pain and my love, and I'll drink away your suffering," Lady Calie whispered.

In the face of such unrepentant hunger, Mary Ellen's romantic notion quickly fled. Brooding, self-tortured, but irredeemably evil: Calie in her tight, many-belted black jumpsuit, an unconscious glare of sin blotching her perfect features. Mary Ellen looked upon the daughter of Lilith and found at the base of all that yearning for passion no real love at all; only a desperate void so painful and all-consuming its owner and victim would commit any atrocity to momentarily still its swirling horror.

She opened her mouth to denounce her suitor; to damn her,

to drive her away.

Before a single syllable could fall from her lips, the room was illuminated by a diffuse but painfully bright blue light, turning Calie's suddenly terrified face the colour of Arctic ice.

XXVI

the manifestation stunned both human and Feeder; the greatest of the archangels had arrived, summoned somehow by the turn of events. The haunter of Lady Calie's dreams; the brother to Mary Ellen's visions over the last few weeks. Michael. The right hand of the Lord.

Unlike Haniel and Nathaniel, Michael chose not to reveal himself in the form he took before God.

Instead, he had discovered a convenient if mean vessel, freshly-emptied.

It was the body of the thing that had masqueraded as the adolescent schoolgirl that Mary Ellen had seen briefly across the ballroom floor before Calie had spirited it away and, presumably, destroyed it. Another of the Feeders Calie had betrayed in her need and desire to possess a human woman. To possess Mary Ellen.

Though it had been a frightful, undead thing before, now it was an abomination of awe-inspiring proportions, a roughly animated, garishly malevolent puppet controlled by a great, unimaginable force with inscrutable intentions.

Light was pouring out of the corpse's eye sockets, and her pale fingertips twitched at an inhumanly spastic rate that made it appear as though there were far more than a mere ten of them, and all scrabbling at the air with gigantic need and unknowable fury.

"My, Tyra, how you've changed," deadpanned Lady Calie.

"Sabbathiel," Mary Ellen murmured to herself. It was only one of the many names that suggested themselves to her. If this thing had been named Tyra once, it seemed the previous occupant had been evicted, and replaced by the lord of angels.

The reanimated creature turned to look at Mary Ellen, gifting her with an awful grin that showed off the blood between her teeth.

Accompanied by the pungent tang of burning metal, a large, thick phallus that danced and glowed as if made out of solid flame materialised at the tip of the isosceles triangle that began at the young girl's narrow hips, growing right through the smudged-dark plaid skirt. The filthy wool began to smoulder, insinuating its crisp odour into the stale nightclub air.

The broken neck of the murdered succubus was still at an awkward angle, but as Mary Ellen watched, the new owner rebalanced the tipped-over coffee oval of Tyra's head in a casually graceful gesture, despite the audible grinding of powdering neck bone.

The reanimated Feeder advanced confidently on Calie, with the same casual contempt as a lion stalking an antelope.

And Calie, evil, implacable, invincibly ancient Calie, was paralysed with terror.

The Feeder mule was leaning back against the emergency exit door, with the concrete steps that led outdoors and up to the alley a tantalising few inches away. She was obviously desperate to flee but unable to, her narrow eyes rolled back, mesmerised by the angel's blinding emanations, the pink sparks dancing around the blue gleam of its etheric cock.

Mary Ellen wondered if "Tyra's" black soul was able to watch heaven's inadvertent justice on its behalf from whatever hellfire pit it now wallowed in.

Swaggering up to Calie, the schoolgirl swivelled its gaze upward to meet the slightly taller woman. A sparkling geyser erupted from the possessed sex demon's fat black-cherry mouth, forcing its way between Calie's equally lush, lipstick-smeared lips, peeling them back so roughly they began to bleed.

Tyra caught Calie's hips up and raised her entirely off the floor; the inhuman domina's legs sought purchase with the graceful, panicked fragility of a spider, but to no avail.

The schoolgirl smiled, her gums radiating an indigo light. The leather jumpsuit with the many buckles that Calie was wearing began to wither away on her body, drying up like a pool of ink under a sun lamp, revealing the full, dark curves of the Feeder's hips.

Calie's terror was palpable to Mary Ellen; in it she tasted a bitter echo of the sins her own father had committed against her. Tyra's vibrating hand moved between Calie's thighs, which muffled a subsequent and truly obscene sound, akin to the butcher's heavy, many-toothed hammer tenderising the meat.

Calie's head whipped from side to side, her long, rough tresses forming cartoon sine waves in the air. Her eyes rolled back in agony, her mouth stretched so wide it seemed about to rip. Leaking from the pores of his horse, Michael's blue radiance played across his victim's face, and her writhing limbs cast swaying forests of shadow against the stone walls.

"Help me, help me *please*, don't, don't, don't, *don't*," Lady Calie gasped, now seeking Mary Ellen's gaze, begging for her intercession.

Embarrassed, disgusted, Mary Ellen looked away for a moment, and then back. But it was too late. Calie's eyes had gone shut, squeezing out trickles of black tears that ran up her cheeks and into her ears, diverted by the spiralling lobes into a vanishing whirlpool.

Michael put both small, ebony hands on her squat, generous hips and simultaneously drew her down even as he thrust his more slim, girlish hips forward so that the mighty flaming dick penetrated Lady Calie swiftly and mercilessly.

Her scream was not in the range of human hearing. Mary Ellen felt a sudden wet stream in her left ear.

It felt like he fucked her forever, but Mary Ellen knew it was only thirty strokes. She counted, hypnotised. Electrified. Horribly fascinated.

At the twenty-sixth stroke, the corpse of the demon schoolgirl had begun to tremble and jerk, announcing an oncoming resolution of the unimaginably apocalyptic coupling.

On the back swing of the twenty-ninth, Michael made the spare ass of his mount arch back an excruciating extra inch, bucking prettily so that the dark flesh split the seam of the torn plaid skirt.

Then he came.

And Calie exploded.

The very flesh fled her bones, in sheer wet sprays of green and violet fluids that drenched half the boiler room. For a brief, impossible instant her skeleton, flinty and naked, hung suspended in the air above Michael. Then it all came tumbling down into his lap, a broken puzzle made up of the fossils of some extinct species.

Calie's head, however, escaped whole, blasted free by one of the many exploding tongues of the prince of angels' orgasm, rocketing in a lazy arc that took it above Mary Ellen's head. It met the wall behind her with a dull, wet *thud*. Mary Ellen was

struck by the need to turn around and look, to see the gruesome trophy, but was afraid to see those almond eyes, turned
up in lost beseechment.

She did, anyway.

And Lady Calie spoke to her, one last time.

Her disembodied head lay on the stained concrete, snake-
like nerves and muscles dangling from the truncated throat.
Her flesh had erupted in dry, concave scales, and her lips were
black and desiccated. Eyes yellow with black slivers for pupils.
You could see the loose vocal cords vibrate with each painful,
barely audible syllable. Mary Ellen didn't know how she could
even hear her voice, with no lungs to power it.

"*Dream...of me ...martyr.*"

Calie's ravaged mouth went slack the moment the last syllable painfully crawled free. A few inches above, those inhuman
pupils revolved once and were still.

Now the head began to steam as if it were broiling, actually
cooking right there before her. In an unnaturally short time,
it had smouldered down into a rough, evil-looking ash, so
much white and grey slag.

Her hands drawn to her breast in shock, Mary Ellen welcomed nausea. Wondering if she were about to faint, she realised
that her fingers felt cool, in contrast to the rest of her flesh.

She shivered as what felt like snowflakes struck her chest
and melted. Glanced down, and saw the holy blood. Again. It
felt more like a disease than a gift of power. Still, just as when
you entered into an intimate engagement with a disease, Mary
Ellen's stigmata was mingling with her essence, directing her
how to feel. Soothing her. Steeling her. Taking control of her
entire corporeal form, rearranging atoms and rerouting nervous system response.

The unannounced orgasm was so tremendous that Mary
Ellen fell back in a helpless fit. She thought she could see the

angel laughing at her, as its dark flesh disintegrated to reveal the terrible and holy true form that grew so large it became an insubstantial blue haze that filled the basement, now turning translucent before finally disappearing altogether.

When Michael was gone Mary Ellen was left alone, beneath the earth, with the ravaged corpses of monsters.

XXVII

*t*he pink luminescence filtered from the direction of the East River, adding an other-worldly cast to the fading Manhattan night. Mary Ellen's boots crunched against the brittle asphalt peeling up from the roof, scuffing up prickly echoes that sounded as if they could cut skin.

When she had revived from her faint, and found herself in the basement room with the grisly remains of the ogre cop and two five-pointed heaps of sickeningly pungent, evil-looking ash, she let her animal instinct take over.

Seeking the open air instead of the shadow world of that dark, close charnel dungeon, Mary Ellen was still too shaken to brave the club and its bizarre, vampiric crowd of desperate revellers, or to subject herself to the crowded embrace of the street, and be swallowed between the tall, foreboding loft buildings of this Midtown neighbourhood. She needed to feel the sky on all sides of her, in a clear and honest embrace.

So she had stumbled up the emergency stairs, hands brushing against walls made red under the ghostly light of the battery-powered emergency lanterns. Michael's visitation seemed to have disrupted the building's doubtlessly ancient wiring — probably sub-code but bribed to pass inspection.

From up here on the roof she could see that his presence had a much more profound result. Though the endless lights of Manhattan stood steadfast in the distance as always, the immediate area had gone into an eclipse: dark rectangles around her and snuffed streetlights below. The blackout had affected at least the surrounding block.

At least the weeping of her stigmata had checked itself. But the flesh of her palms still throbbed in a deep rhythm that mocked her place in the universe, that trumpeted the mean methods by which heaven and hell were conducting their sly, passionate struggles.

What have I ever done, Mary Ellen wondered numbly, *to deserve this*?

She'd been drafted as an unfortunate bystander into a role caught between two flailing, merciless armies, each so sweetly hateful of the other that any concern over inadvertent casualties was neglected. Whether titularly Good or Evil, these soldiers battled for body and soul.

She shivered all the way down to her cunt as she thought of the weird, awful thrill that had come from witnessing Calie being fucked into non-existence by unforgiving Michael, the legendary right hand of God. The horrible truth was that the sight had been more provocative than the most forbidden pornography of which the human brain could conceive. A nightmarish wet dream that would stay with her forever; she knew that from now on, every time she felt her body roused to wakefulness, a shard of that apocalyptic orgasm would resurface and dig into her thoughts, like a sliver of glass lodged just under the skin.

Which provoked the question: Was that what she desired? Or was she better off safe in her mantle of numbness?

Her contemplations were interrupted by a chill breeze wafting across the rooftop from somewhere in the direction of Brooklyn, its insinuating touch raising goosebumps on her naked arms.

A nausea of her entire body resulted, all her nerve endings activated into a symphony of prickles and jolts — as if she were in the path of the faint echo from some impossibly huge generator, a vast and dark machine capable of propelling its charge not just for miles, but for light years, out into the solar system, out to the cold and empty stars.

The inadequate, inaccurate human terms for the energy she felt were many: Evil, Satan, sin, corruption. Brushed by the faintest tendril of an unseen leviathan, she twitched and gulped in revulsion.

Mary Ellen dropped into a squat, her arms wrapped across her belly, ready and by this time quite willing to vomit.

At least it was less far for her to fall to the tar paper in the next moment, when that initial surge was answered by a great wave of power that her senses obliquely translated as being wet and green, coming back in answer from somewhere in the other direction. Somewhere up, someplace in the far desolate galaxies that mankind has given up trying to reach with anything but stupid mechanical toys thrown up in the air on expensive but Quixotic whim. It was not merely an answer. It was The Answer.

Before she could get her heels back underneath her, the power and the glory seized Mary Ellen Masters in a rough, merciless caress, pushing back the lids of her eyes until she stared twitching and sightless up into the funnel of night, gaze burned blind by a ghost radiance emanating from a wet, distant vastness that constantly exploded within itself, reshaping through a never-resting process of growth and decay, multiple artifices embroidering in ornate cancers across a membrane that began and ended at unimaginably distant poles.

Her soul filled with alien fire. A rapacious, all-consuming love that eradicated every shred of her individuality, overloading and burning out bundles of neurons used prior only for the transport of the discreet electrical charge of her own thoughts, the organisation of her unconscious logic and emotions.

If her entire identity amounted to little more than a molecule, then she was in the presence of an entity the size of the sun, an immeasurable thing broiling and crackling with white flames, decorated with dark spots that radiated an intolerable heat.

The sensation was unbearable. She tried by the force of her will to make her body numb and impervious to the rough seduction, instead focusing every shred of her conscious thought and physical energy on her lungs and throat, pushing up and out a raw, drawn-out scream of rebellion.

In a moment of perfect knowledge, she understood it was the same noise that Jesus had made at the moment he realised himself forsaken, and Judas, silver burning his palm, upon learning he had been impassively manipulated by the diffident architect of a faith squalling to be born.

It was the discreet but final pop of the vessels bursting in Mohammed's brain, painting red flowers against the sudden darkness as he was overtaken by the knowledge that he truly would not be allowed to see the holy land he had suffered for. The sullen crackle of Prometheus's nervous system bathing in the unbearable white flames of his liver regenerating.

She took the Lord's name in vain: "FUUUCK YOUUU," she wailed, or at least those were the words she strived to get out. As the crushing wave of His love receded from her shore, the void that remained was filled in by an onrushing despair. Now she knew the truth beyond any doubt, or lack of faith:

His gift, once given, was not subject to return or exchange.

She didn't know whether to find a Bible or hack off her hands at the wrists. At her back, Sunday morning finally rose, and she could feel all the dominions behind her, waiting expectantly to greet their new vessel.

Available now from

Passengers

Sue Lightfoot

An unusual affair. On the commuter train to London the
passengers are the same every day, but they remain strangers who
never speak, never touch, who even avoid looking at each other.

Nikolaus only knows the woman from the plastic name-badge
she wears — Cassie. That is all he knows about her. But he wants
her more than anything he has ever wanted. Cassie sees him
every morning on the train. Sometimes she thinks she
catches him looking at her.

The affair that develops between Cassie and Nikolaus is
all-consuming. Little by little their desires are liberated from
any kind of restraint or inhibition. But is their passion
really what it seems? Could something so intense be no
more than a double fantasy?

Available now from

 EROS✝

The Safety of Unknown Cities

Lucy Taylor

In search of transcendence, Val Petrillo makes a perilous journey to North Africa in search of a magical city where all one's sexual yearnings can come to life. In the vastness of the forbidden continent, she ends up finding more than she expected in a world of unbridled sexuality and rampant horror.

Ghoulish, pyrotechnic and lascivious, this is a stunning first novel of erotic horror by the field's most sensuous exponent since Anne Rice.

MAIL ORDER

All Eros Plus titles are available through most good
bookshops or direct from our Eros Plus mail order service.
Telephone 01536 763 631 with your credit card details or send
the coupon below to Eros Plus Mail Order, PO Box 54,
Desborough, Northants., NN14 2UH. All titles are £5.99 plus
75 pence per book for postage and packing.
Order four books or more and the post and packing is free.

The Best of the Journal of Erotica	Jakubowski (Ed.)	(6357)
Maya 29	Alice Joanou	(6349)
The Ties that Bind	Vanessa Duriès	(6330)
Dark Matter	Michael Perkins	(6365)
The Watcher & the Watched	Michael Crawley	(6403)
Reclining Nude	Claudia Riess	(7000)
Passengers	Sue Lightfoot	(7019)
The Safety of Unknown Cities	Lucy Taylor	(7221)

Name

Date

Address

Postcode

Please send me the following book/s (fill in the product codes of the book/s you wish to order)

*I enclose a cheque/postal order (made payable to Titan Books Ltd) for £

*Please debit my Visa/Access/Amex card for £

Expiry Date

Signature

We aim to supply your order within 5 working days, however, please allow a maximum of 28 days for delivery.
ITB/PB (*delete as appropriate)